ZEN IN THE ART OF SLAYING VAMPIRES

25TH ANNIVERSARY AUTHOR REVISED EDITION

STEVEN-ELLIOT ALTMAN

WFP

eBook ISBN: 978-1-68057-189-9
Trade Paperback ISBN: 978-1-68057-188-2
Hardcover ISBN: 978-1-68057-190-5
Hardcover Case Bind ISBN: 978-1-68057-256-8

Cover design and illustrations by Alexandre Rito
Additional artwork by Leah Ryan
Kevin J. Anderson, Art Director
Published by
WordFire Press, LLC
PO Box 1840
Monument CO 80132
Kevin J. Anderson & Rebecca Moesta, Publishers
WordFire Press eBook Edition 2021
WordFire Press Trade Paperback Edition 2021
WordFire Press Hardcover Edition 2021
Printed in the USA

Join our WordFire Press Readers Group for
sneak previews, updates, new projects, and giveaways.
Sign up at wordfirepress.com

AN INTRODUCTION:

WHAT THIS STORY IS ACTUALLY ABOUT

BY NANCY HOLDER

When Steve invited me to write the introduction to the 25th anniversary reissue of *Zen in the Art of Slaying Vampires*, he included a note that read, "Can't wait to hear what the story is actually about. I have faith you'll see it." And he was right.

Jung said, "The man who has not passed through the inferno of his passions has never overcome them." And he was wrong.

This is a novel that takes you through the inferno without flinching, but with deep compassion. It's a perfect novel for our times, when so many of us see no way to douse the flames of fear, hatred, and despair. How to deal with them, these raging human passions? What if we never can?

"What's the worst that can happen?" we often teasingly ask when urging a friend or lover to take action. The implication, of course, is that the worst can't be all that bad, or that the outcome our friend is envisioning is too horrific to transpire. As soon as we began to discuss *Zen*, Steve and I bonded: we know about the worst—*our* worst—because it is the same, and it has already happened to both of us.

Death came for our parents way too early in life and left us orphans. Our safe places were gone. We were upended. We were left. Grief of that magnitude is never overcome. What Steve tells us in *Zen* is that grief doesn't have to be overcome, nor should it be. And then he tells us what to do with it instead.

This novel—part memoir, part handbook, wrapped in the cape of vampirism—burns with passion and longing fomented from personal knowledge of the Worst. With raw unselfconsciousness, and humble honesty, it traces the journey of David Patterson, the narrator, as he assays Zen Buddhism shortly before he makes the dark descent into a vampiric existence. For him, this is the worst that can happen. Death—early death—is not beautiful. Being a vampire is ugly. It is not Anne Rice's Lestat or the Edward of *Twilight*. It is cruel and mean and disgusting, as addiction and unbridled demand always are. If, as Clive Barker asserts, we are all books of blood, vampires are unspeakable tragedies.

Through the drinking of blood, the theft of another's *prana*—life force—is what *Zen*'s vampires demand. Insatiable. Unrelenting. Yet Patterson's devotion to the Way—to the Buddhist tradition of restraint at all times and in all things—transforms him from a commonplace bloodsucker into a unique, singular figure: possibly as one who has traveled the karmic wheel in these same cycles before, to arrive at a crossroads now. Allying himself with humanity—what he believes he once was—he moves along the path of choice: to protect humans, he must kill vampires, while experiencing psychic wounding so deep that reality shifts repeatedly. Time circles, he relives his agony: wishing cannot make it so. It can never make it so. Death is death, no matter whose death it is.

Working with that material would result in a fine horror novel, but *Zen* goes deeper. The pain—the gaze of the horror reader—is honored; but order is not restored and nihilism is not celebrated. What happens instead is that the narrator— and his creator—both accept the mantel and mantra of the *bodhisattva*, one whose self-enlightenment requires a higher response. This manifests in the story as a specific, repeated phrase, which I can't repeat here or I will do the work that the novel requires of you.

Steve's father died in the aftermath of a plane crash, and his mother from cancer. He was a son of death. After both his parents were gone, he worked as a grief counselor with terminal hospice patients and studied Tibetan Buddhist meditation and healing with Robert Thurman (Uma Thurman's father), who said to him, "I don't want you to become Buddhist—I just want you to be Buddha." As Steve himself will allow, he didn't experience the act of writing this book. What he did was embody direct self-expression, becoming an artistic act, and that act was this book—ignited by the forces of grief and youth, that raw, early power that some writers tame and others ride. Gored by the reality that the worst *can* happen, that it does, and that it did, and might again (no immunity is bestowed on those already visited), he created out of himself a fearless story wrapped in fear—fear of attack, of loss, of pain and shame. It's not surprising that some script writers on my beloved *Buffy the Vampire Slayer* have told Steve that the novel was an important part of their arsenal, and that friends and colleagues consider this book ("flawed as it may be," he adds) his most important work. Others have recognized its quality: it has been optioned for film three times, with attachments such as directors John Landis (*An American Werewolf in London*), Renny Harlin (*The Long Kiss Goodnight*) and Russell Mulcahy (*Highlander*), and stars James Franco, Britney Spears, Justin Timberlake, and Lindsay Lohan.

What he—and by extension, his avatar, the narrator David Patterson—does with the knowledge that the worst perpetually hovers, results in a revelation, a Way forward, past the koan of The Worst. It has to do with why Jung is wrong, and it's a mandate for living that Patterson isn't sure his fellows will ultimately believe and accept. But I know that it's what Steve believes and accepts, and that he hopes his readers will do likewise, to their benefit, as they navigate their journey through the messiness that is life—not a tragedy, but a real story, fully realized and fully lived for each second that life is. I number myself among Steve's friends, colleagues, and admirers who say yes, this is his most important work. It answers my despair over these times, these years, and this adult child's lifelong yearning for arms that were not there. I believe it will answer the despair of others.

And I thank him sincerely for having written it.

—Nancy Holder
Near Seattle, July 19, 2020

DEDICATION

*Dedicated in loving memory to Kevin R. Bailey
and Gregory P. Naudus*

*Special thanks to the entire Thomas family, Patrick Merla, Mindy
Yale, Leslie Burns Patience, Sari Daugherty, and Dawn Emery
Thorne, all of whom having selflessly offered their tireless
encouragement and having made a difference in my life, and
especially in this work.*

For I can not find a man,
Though that I walked into India,
Neither in a city nor in a village,
That would exchange his youth for mine age;
And therefore must I have mine age still,
As long a time as is God's will.
Nor Death, alas, will not have my life.
Thus walk I, like a wrestless captive,
And on the ground which is my mother's gate,
I knock with my staff, both early and late,
And say, "Dearest mother, let me in!
See how I vanish, flesh and blood and skin!"

Chaucer
The Pardoner's Tale

The light of the eye is as a comet,
And Zen's activity is as lightning.
The sword that kills the man
Is the sword that saves the man.

Zen Master Ekai

A Buddhist monk looks in the mirror and sees no reflection. What conclusion might he draw? That he's either a master, a vampire ... or both.

Anonymous

1

Why Zen?

Mankind has been slaying these abominations, these blasphemous transformations of his kin, since time immemorial, so why now do we turn toward Zen, the Eastern *Way*, as our modern method of slaying the *un*dead? We turn to Zen because the act of slaying a killer, however justifiable in the case of any particular vampire, should still be viewed as a decimation of life, and is therefore detrimental to the spiritual growth of the slayer himself.

Time was when vampires had little to fear but the occasional enlightened soul who could muster a torch-wielding mob to their tombs before sunset. Modern society has learned the signs indicating the vampire's presence: puncture wounds on a corpse, an inexplicable amount of blood loss, a culprit riddled with bullets who can rise and flee police.

Unfortunately, the vampire has been glamorized by novels and the film industry to the point where communal awareness is insufficient defense. The death toll continues rising, the causes too often recorded as natural. Yet many still resist believing vampires truly exist, even when faced with insurmountable evidence. They risk becoming prey.

The Way of Zen requires that seekers overhaul their lives to achieve self-awareness. He who would master the Way of Zen in the Art of Slaying Vampires faces these trials as well, with the added assurance of continuous mortal jeopardy.

Why then, should anyone attempt to master this Art?

First, any Art within the realm of man's imagination is in itself of divine origin and therefore worth mastering.

Second, without Masters of the Art to stop vampires from transforming the general public, humankind could become the minority in this struggle, with little more freedom than sheep in a slaughterhouse.

The essence of the situation is, of course, blood. Being a vampire, being human, life and death, health and weakness —all depend on the ebb and flow of blood, the River of Life. Blood contains both physical and metaphysical, natural and supernatural properties. Blood type is determined genetically and spiritually at conception through the merging lifeforces of the parents. The blood in your veins is being purified and reproduced at all times, carrying within it your lifeforce and the potential to spread itself.

A vampire is basically a parasite, capable of extracting and transforming human lifeforce into vampiric lifeforce by sucking out the human's blood then forcing—or in some cases allowing—the human to ingest some of the blood back.

Human females menstruate in lunar cycles as affirmation of their ability to create life. Vampire females no longer possess this capability. This seemingly obvious difference is important. Vampires can only reproduce through premeditated murder.

But have you considered what is happening metaphysically during this transformation?

The human is in the course of natural spiritual development, incurring and paying off karmic debts and lessons among fellow travelers, when suddenly the course is violently disrupted by a form of psychic rape, contaminating the human's lifeforce like a virus. If you're lucky, they just kill you and leave your body to rot. If not, you awake to intense psychic distress and physical pain, with a hunger that can only be quenched by the blood of another human being.

I myself made no conscious decision to slay vampires, although a Master once told me, moments after we met, he divined that my entire life had been preparing me for this vocation. The seven piles of ash surrounding him at that meeting attested to his own mastery of the Art. I never laid eyes on him again, and I'm still not sure if I believe what he said.

I was subsequently chosen by the Masters to write this introductory work, though I haven't gone through the training I'm about to relate. I don't hunt as the Masters hunt, nor slay as the Masters slay. I arrived at my present level of expertise as the result of an obscene accident.

I suffer from a rather rare, perhaps singular affliction, and my methodology differs from that of any other vampire slayer. It is through this affliction, for reasons unknown to me, that the Masters wish you, the Aspirant, to be introduced to the Art of Slaying Vampires.

2

You see, I myself am a Vampire.

But don't jump to any conclusions, they'll all be wrong. You'll come to see that calling myself a vampire is somewhat misleading.

The Masters are humans, full flesh and blood. I am the sole exception. It's a common joke among Aspirants that of course it "takes one to know one." But there's nothing I wouldn't do to make it otherwise. All things considered—I'd much rather be dead. Truly dead. But putting that aside, at least for the duration of our time together, I hope my condition will indeed serve you all as a useful lens with which to examine the subject.

Let's begin the course of instruction by observing several easily identifiable physical changes that occur shortly after a human body has been subdued; they are:

1. A paleness or bluish tint to the skin due to oxygen depletion of the blood.
2. Enlarged canine teeth.

3. No heartbeat.

4. Unnatural hardening and thickening of the fingernails and toenails.

5. No respiration, i.e. rising and falling of the chest.

6. Eyes fixed fully dilated, often discolored.

7. Unnatural lightness of step, as evidenced by a lack of depth to a footprint.

These are the more obvious clues to primary identification that can be utilized without the use of a laboratory; however, be advised that a skilled vampire will be adept at concealing these physical attributes. For example, a vampire who has recently fed shall be filled with the lifeforce of another, whereby paleness of skin may be temporarily metamorphosed to a ruddy glow of health. The fingernails may be trimmed or the hands gloved. Dark glasses or colored contact lenses may be utilized and breathing is easily simulated. On that last note, I suggest that during meditation you pay strict attention to the rhythm of your own breathing, so as to distinguish the true breath from the fictitious. "Know thyself and thou shalt know thine enemy. Know thine enemy and thou shalt know thyself."

Let me illustrate for you the field practicality of these primary identifiers by relating an actual hunt in which I engaged during my years in association with the Ministry—an organization you may not be familiar with, rightfully so—a worldwide network of occult watchtowers standing sentinel over humankind. Rest assured that without them, I would not be writing this guide, and you would be living in a much less civilized society.

A report was received at the New York headquarters, where I had been stationed, that several related kidnappings and one confirmed murder had occurred in Birchrunville, Pennsylvania, a small town about forty miles outside of Philadelphia. The murder victim, a fifteen-year-old girl, was suspected of having been a member of a local satanic cult. The Ministry is notified immediately of any event suggesting occult activity. They sent me to investigate, on loan to the Philadelphia office. I arrived in Birchrunville by train soon after nightfall.

To describe the town as "in the middle of nowhere" would be ascribing it too specific a locality. As is often the case, I wasn't well received at the sheriff's office. Already spooked by the Ministry sending someone, indicating they were dealing with a potentially paranormal situation, they were totally unprepared for who they got. I can be pretty disturbing, although I employ the latest cosmetic advances to veil my true nature, wear colored contact lenses, am adept at concealing my eyeteeth during conversation, and control the speed of my movements and pitch of my voice. I kept my collar high and my hat brim low.

The sheriff, a tall, rugged man with a pockmarked face, kept his distance, clearly unhappy to have me poking my nose in his district. I knew his type. He wanted this over with as soon as possible. He'd submit to my direction under duress, but not personally. That would have been too much for his ego.

He assigned a deputy to me.

Jones was thirty-something, fair-haired, and nervous as hell when we shook hands. He took me to the morgue to examine the corpse.

The marks on the girl were undeniably vampire-induced: five sets of puncture wounds—three on the neck, one on the left breast, and one on the inner right thigh.

Jones pointed out a small spider tattoo on the back of the girl's left earlobe.

"What kind of sick individual could do something like this?" he said.

"Nothing *human* did this," I said. "And there was more than one of them. These puncture wounds don't all match. At least three of them aren't the same diameter across the length of the bite. The one on the breast is partially healed. It occurred several days before the other four, suggesting the victim had previous involvement with her assailants, perhaps willingly, before she was murdered. We're dealing with a coven of vampires."

Jones paled.

"Can you handle that, deputy?"

He looked very unhappy but inclined his head, apparently unable to speak. I decided to occupy him with a concrete task.

"I'll need the files on each of the other four children immediately. And Jones, as my liaison, nothing I say in your presence is ever to be repeated. Do you understand?"

"But the sheriff—"

I cut him off, subtly flashing my eyeteeth.

"Don't question my instructions. There's no time for it if we want to save these children. Your sheriff has traces of cocaine beneath his left index fingernail. I don't trust him, which means you don't trust him either now."

Jones shook his head, bewildered, but agreed.

"Good. Now collect those files for me, find us an unmarked car, and take me to the scene where the girl was found."

Jones and I proceeded to an abandoned warehouse on

State Road 401. Crossing the police barricades, we found the entrance padlocked.

"Is this a police seal?" I asked.

"It's not ours," Jones replied.

I turned my back to Jones, tore out the lock, and was nearly overcome by the stench that greeted me—a recently abandoned den. Jones was better off, being unable to sense the aftershocks of death.

At the center of the huge room was a stone altar, drenched with the blood of several sacrificial victims. Everyone's blood varies in shade to the supernatural eye. At first glance, I noted at least eleven variations.

A search of the warehouse revealed two items of interest. The first was a fine strand of yellow hair matching the description of one of the missing teens, a fourteen-year-old boy, with jagged traces of scalp attached, indicating the strand had been torn from the boy's head while he was dragged by the hair. By the smell of it, he'd smoked marijuana regularly. I concluded from the scent of the remaining oil on the strand he'd been relatively uninjured at the time of losing the hair.

The second item was a crumpled note Jones discovered wedged into a crevice of the altar: a band flyer with a hand-written message scrawled on the back.

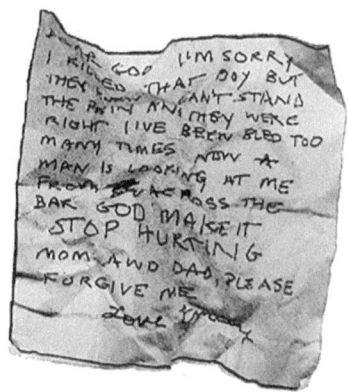

I pocketed the note and we left the scene twenty-two minutes and thirty-seven seconds before sunrise.

We both got a good day's sleep, and I awoke the next evening with the same cycle of denial-anger-self-loathing I usually wake up to. And as usual, I got myself past it with a brief meditation. I telephoned Jones, issued him my orders, and then pulled on some ratty jeans and a leather jacket. Jones arrived punctually at my hotel, and we headed out. It was late Autumn and the air was cool and crisp enough to display his breath. There was a waking gibbous moon high overhead.

I asked if there were any developments during the day; there were none. Per my instructions he'd made up a list of all the local nightclubs, with asterisks by the four within a ten-mile radius featuring live music. Dance clubs with their young, turnable prey, are always a good place to start.

"Can I shoot one of these things, if we find them?" asked Jones, as we drove along a steep dirt road.

"You can't kill them with bullets," I said.

"Terrific," he muttered. "Just how strong are they?"

"A vampire is as strong as the amount of blood it has

stolen. Unfed, they're about as strong as they were when alive. A vampire drunk on the blood of ten men has the strength of ten men, but only until the blood wanes."

"This is crazy," he said. "Don't you find this crazy?"

"I'm not a psychiatrist. I just slay vampires."

"Great line of work," he said, and lit a cigarette. "You know, I'm not sure what's screwing me up worse, the fact they really exist, or that you do."

"I'm not sure either."

"Yeah, well. Have you got a name I might call you?"

Apart from the dozen or so IDs in my wallet, I had no name. I pointed ahead.

"Is that the first club on the list?"

"Yeah. Rathbones."

"Pull over here."

We pulled to the side of the road with the front door to the bar in full view and doused the lights. I rolled down my window and tasted the brittle air.

"Does it have to be human blood?" Jones said.

"What?" I said, unsure what he was asking.

"The blood they drink. Could it be cows' blood or chickens' blood?"

"No."

"Why not?"

"Let's say you were in an accident and lost a great deal of blood and needed a transfusion. The doctors couldn't very well give you chicken blood, could they? Not compatible. It's like that with them, too."

Just then two of the bastards drove into the parking lot in a red Buick Skylark, spewing gravel.

"There," I indicated.

"Are you sure?"

"Yes. See how pale they are? They haven't fed yet, which is to our advantage. Let them go inside, twenty-count head start. That way we'll see if they've come to feed or make a contact."

My senses were immediately assaulted when we entered the bar after them. Lights flared and dazzled; acid rock music pulsed in harsh vibrations, shaking the concrete building foundations. And, wafting up like a dark cloud, the scent of vampire. They'd separated; one was at the bar speaking to a red-haired girl, the other was nowhere in sight.

"I'll take him," I whispered to Jones. "You grab the girl. She's human."

I waded through the dancing bodies, moved in behind him. Sensing me, he spun around, fangs bared, in an offensive stance. Jones grabbed the girl and hurried her into the crowd. The vampire was young when he was turned—confused, frightened, angry. Under a leather jacket, his shirt was open to the waist. Inside him, beneath the overwhelming bloodlust, deeper than his fear as he tried to fathom who and what I was, I felt a glimmer of something worth saving.

He lunged.

I sidestepped, tripping him and sending him crashing to the floor. In an instant, he was up and at me again, swinging wildly. His sharp nails caught the left side of my face, breaking the skin below the cheek. Of course, no blood came. I smashed my bare left hand hard against his exposed chest.

He screamed, went down on his haunches, his back against the bar, looking past me in blind terror.

Crouching, I took his head in my hands and made him look at me.

"Don't be frightened," I said. "This is your chance for redemption. Tell me where the children are."

But he was already gone, his heightened senses snapping off one by one like internal circuit breakers.

I scanned the club for his companion. Unable to detect him, I bolted out the door and was surprised to find the second vampire pinned to the ground beneath the front wheel of the squad car, trying to claw his way free. The girl's body lay broken in the dirt. A small drunken crowd was slowly forming. Jones was covered in blood, not his own, standing just out of the vampire's flailing range, his gun aimed at its head.

"What happened?" I asked, stepping up to him.

"Sonofabitch ambushed me when I got to the car. Threw me aside and then ... *Mother of God.* He ripped out her insides while she just looked at me. I shot him once and he laughed. So I got in the car and ran over the bastard."

"Good work, Jones. Radio this in. I'll take care of him."

As Jones went for the radio, I knelt out of range of the vampire. He'd ceased thrashing and lay staring anxiously up at me.

"Any last requests?" I said.

He bared his fangs and struggled to reach me, but the car was too heavy.

"Set me free!" he hissed.

"Where are the children?"

"Set me free and I'll tell you."

"Tell me and I'll set you free."

"They're at Jacobs' Mill. Now set me free, you freak."

I slapped his face—hard—then lifted up the front end of the car. (Jones had just got out and was crouching by the girl, his back to me.) The vampire rose, dusted the dirt off his jeans.

"She wasn't your type," he sniggered, smiling evilly down at Jones.

Jones looked about ready to discharge his firearm again when a piercing scream inside the bar shattered the air. The music stopped. Everyone turned.

"That was your friend," I told the vampire. "Taking his own life. When I touch someone who's infected, as I touched you a moment ago ..."

His smile faded. He sped off down the road in a blur. Jones gaped at the sight.

"No need to go after him," I said, opening the driver's-side car door. "He's done for. We need to get to a place called Jacobs' Mill as quickly as possible. The children are there."

"How do you know?"

"That one just told me."

"How do you know he was telling the truth?"

"Truth has a very distinctive sound."

"I know a quick way."

Jones slid in on the passenger side and radioed the station, requesting backup to meet us at the Mill. Ten minutes later, we arrived to discover an abandoned police car already parked in front of the building. Jones said it belonged to a fellow deputy named McNerney.

Jones drew his gun. We entered the mill with extreme caution, moving through darkness toward rustling noises coming from a back office. Swinging the door wide, we found Deputy McNerney, lifting a child's unconscious body. Three other children were bound and gagged on the floor, two of them still alive. McNerney turned.

"How'd you manage to beat us here?" Jones asked him.

McNerney just stood there, staring at me.

"He's not human, Jones," I said.

"Are you crazy? I've known this man all my life."

"There's no condensation. He's *not* breathing."

McNerney reached down, unlatched his holster, and whipped his gun into a blur of motion. He and Jones began firing simultaneously.

Two bullets struck me, sending me backward through the door. McNerney and Jones emptied their remaining rounds into each other. By the time I got back into the room they both lay twisted, wet, and broken. I moved to the vampire first, laying my bare hand against him. He convulsed. Assured he was no longer a threat, I turned to Jones. He was trying to raise himself off the floor.

The kids fought their gags with muffled screams. Somehow the boy McNerney had been carrying had avoided further injury. Sirens were fast approaching in the distance.

"Did any of you drink their blood at any point?" I asked the three surviving teens as I heard cars pull up outside.

They swore they hadn't. I untied them, touching my bare skin to theirs one by one as a precaution, then sent them outside to the backup.

Jones had propped himself against a wall and sat bleeding everywhere. There was nothing I could do for him.

"We got three of them," he said, managing a nervous chuckle.

"Yes."

"Tell me something."

"If I can."

"Are you the same damned thing as them?"

He was gone before I could answer.

3

Be forewarned: if you choose to become an Aspirant of the *Way* and encounter a vampire before your training has reached the stage of *satori*, you will certainly perish. The Zen Aspirant resides in a cocoon of constant struggle to master his art, weaponless, defenseless, telegraphing distress —a veritable target for vampires.

Comprehending this truth is the first step on the path for the Aspirant—and the direct placement of his life in mortal jeopardy. If he chooses to continue, he enters a monastery, to dedicate himself entirely to the Art. (In rare instances, the training may occur between Master and pupil in a non-monastic setting.)

Monastery life is hard, often involving years of failure as the Zen Aspirant attempts to cast off the world of delusion and attain enlightenment through rigorous training under the guidance of a Master. Luxury, property, relaxation, recreation, entertainment, comfort—all are absent. There is one goal: Master the Art of Slaying Vampires. All other thoughts must fall to the wayside.

The path to enlightenment employs three states of mind: Great Faith, Great Determination, and Great Skepticism. These states, we are assured, provide sure footing in all endeavors, be they employed in the scaling of mountains or the quest for truth. Aspirant, draw strength from the knowledge your first step upon the path is one of inner recognition and presupposes your potential to walk it successfully, eventually gaining mastery. As with any Art that follows the *Way*, presupposition is key. In Zen Archery, for example, the presupposition is that the unfired arrow has already struck the target; there is no separation between the archer and his goal. A true Master of the Art of Slaying Vampires, having perfected the use of his weapons, need no longer wield them. They need not even be at hand. It is presupposed that they exist and shall strike true. Perhaps this sounds preposterous. You have a weapon but you have no weapon? How is this so?

"It *is* so," the Master replies.

The Aspirant who hasn't yet emptied himself of thought flails and grasps for understanding until, through meditation and discipline, he becomes a vessel to be filled by the Master.

The first goal for which the Aspirant strives is *satori*, a personal awakening or insight into a higher level of awareness. It may take years to attain, a slow dawning; in rare instances, it may arrive abruptly, an instant of sudden enlightenment brought to fruition by a caring and gentle Master. It is not an intellectual process and cannot be faked. A Master can read the aftershocks of *satori* in a student as distinctly as a Richter scale registers earth tremors.

To illustrate:

A Zen Master named Ryutan had a very determined

young pupil named Tokusan who was having great difficulty in his studies. One evening Tokusan sat meditating with the Master for several hours, at the end of which he found himself overflowing with questions. Weary of Tokusan's ramblings, the Master suggested he retire and sleep. Tokusan bowed, opened the screen to the zendo (meditation hall), and noticed it had grown dark outside.

"Please Master," said Tokusan, "allow me some light to guide my way."

Ryutan lit a candle and offered it to his pupil. Tokusan reached out to take it, and the moment it was in his grasp, Ryutan blew the candle out. Instantly, a window was blown open in Tokusan's mind. He achieved *satori*.

You cannot force enlightenment. The student must be ripe for *satori*, having spent a great deal of time learning to master the six immaculate senses: sight, sound, touch, taste, smell, and cognition.

Cognition is often overlooked as a sense in Western thought, or else confused as a culmination of the other five. The student of Zen learns that cognition can occur even when the other senses are disengaged, and can be utilized to know a subject with the same limitations as the other five.

Until you have gained mastery, a vampire will out-sight you, out-hear you, out-touch you, out-taste you, and out-smell you, though its cognition will always be dulled by its drive to siphon others' lifeforce.

The tale of my own first *satori* was instrumental in causing the honorable Master Choi Leung to decide it would be wiser to enlist my services, rather than set me aflame.

I was thirteen years old, living with my parents and younger sister, Chelsea, in a meticulously maintained home in a small town in upstate New York. My father was a professor of English with a predilection for Chaucer at a nearby college, my mother a legal librarian engaged in court research. Our house was filled with books, to the point where a visitor once remarked, "Those bookshelves appear to be holding the house up quite nicely."

Unlike our parents, my sister and I felt stifled living in a library.

We never knew in advance in what room one of them might choose to work. When we got home from school, we'd have to locate them then find someplace to hang out at the opposite end of the house. We spent a lot of time outside during warmer months. If we were inside, our parents posted television hours, subject to change without notice, and the radio volume had to be kept low. Still, we loved our parents, although they found us troublesome at times.

One Saturday, Dad was in his study grading finals papers, a near-religious time with special added observances. Mom was deep in her law books, close to some deadline. It being the weekend, Chelsea and I were off from school.

We were outside playing kick the can with neighborhood kids. The others dropped out of the game one by one as it grew dark, and went home to dinner. Chelsea and I remained outside on the porch for a while, listening to crickets chirping and watching the sunset. With Mom and Dad caught up in their work, we knew dinner wasn't happening anytime soon. It might easily be skipped altogether.

"Looks like it's gonna rain," I said, noticing the clouds moving in.

Chelsea sat, feet dangling off the porch railing, fiddling with one of the straps on the denim coveralls she wore all the time, blonde bangs hanging in unkempt strands into her dauntless blue eyes, the look on her face at once determined and full of yearning. My male friends were already beginning to observe her with lingering glances.

"Let's go inside," she said.

"I don't know ..."

She cut me off, placing her finger gently on my lips then moving it to her own to signal "quiet." We tiptoed into the parlor.

We weren't in the house more than five minutes when Chelsea accidentally broke a glass. A simple, forgotten wineglass from the night before. The crimson contents spilled all over a priceless edition of *The Count of Monte Cristo* that had once belonged to playwright Eugene O'Neill, purchased at auction by my father at tremendous expense.

Dad chose that moment to enter the parlor. Seeing the defiled book, his features in rapid succession registered astonishment, helplessness, and anger that escalated when his gaze fell on Chelsea.

She stiffened before him, laughed nervously—which angered Dad more. I thought he might actually hit her. I felt completely helpless.

"Do you know what you've destroyed?" he roared.

Chelsea just stood there, shifting her weight from side to side.

"It was an accident!" I cried.

Mom came rushing into the parlor, taking in the situation in a glance. She stepped between them, diffusing the confrontation in an instant, then looked after the book to the best of her abilities with a dry cloth. It was decided the family would go out for dinner. Everybody needed a break.

We piled into the family sedan with Dad driving and

Mom in the passenger seat. I sat behind Mom, Chelsea behind Dad. It had begun to rain. Mom made a face at Dad as he took us out of the driveway a little too quickly.

The car fishtailed a few times on the slick roadway as we merged onto the highway. A truck was coming straight toward us.

The next thing I knew, my head was crashing hard against the steel frame of the back of the seat. I vaguely remember seeing blood on Chelsea's chin, and trying to reach my hand out to her. My hand wouldn't move.

Several hours later, Chelsea and I were sitting in a hospital waiting room. I had a pressure bandage around my head the doctor said was just a precaution, while we waited for my X-rays to come back. Chelsea had eleven stitches below her very swollen lower lip. She stared at herself in a mirror.

A flaxen-haired nurse poked her head into the room every five minutes or so, to ask if we were feeling all right. I noticed she had really nice breasts then chastised myself for noticing such a thing at such a time. Once she looked in on us and said we'd been lucky to get "only a little banged up." We didn't feel lucky.

The next time we saw her she was extremely pale. She sat between Chelsea and me and held our hands. Chelsea started crying, even before the nurse told us our father was dead.

She sat with us a while. I remember her kissing Chelsea several times, and rubbing my shoulders in that uncomfortable way strangers attempt to be intimate. I was too shocked to cry, and anyway, Chelsea was crying enough for both of us. The nurse asked if we'd be okay by ourselves while she went to check on our mother's condition. We nodded. She squeezed our hands and left. Chelsea nuzzled into my shoulder, still crying.

Then the nurse was at the door again, and we knew our mother was gone.

The funeral was simple and quick. Chelsea and I were to be shipped out to third cousins we'd never met, in New Mexico. A lady social worker brought us home and helped us pack and crate the family belongings.

I was going through a box of old photographs in the attic when it dawned on me Chelsea and I were now orphans. With our parents gone, I felt I had no business existing. I was sure I'd simply have faded into nothingness if I didn't have Chelsea.

My thoughts were interrupted by a series of loud crashes downstairs. I ran to the living room and found Chelsea hurling books from the shelves, wailing like an animal. Volumes flew in all directions, shattering lamps and windows. When one shelf was emptied, she moved to the next.

The social worker and I watched in silence.

When Chelsea was done, she ran to me and collapsed in my arms, sobbing. I suggested the social worker take a break and come back in a little while. She agreed wholeheartedly.

I sat Chelsea on the couch and stroked her hair until she was calm. Hearing a buzzing sound, I looked up.

It was a yellow jacket. It had probably gotten inside when the social worker failed to close the screen door. It flew past Chelsea and me on the couch once, twice, three times.

Suddenly she was up again, furiously swinging a pillow, trying to kill the yellow jacket, growing increasingly frustrated as she swung and missed, swung and missed, swung and missed.

Watching this sad exercise in futility, I achieved satori. There was no separation between myself and the wasp.

"Don't, Chelsea!" I shouted. "You've got no reason to kill it!"

She dropped the pillow and stared at me, looking stunned.

The yellow jacket slammed itself against the window a few times, attempting to escape. I went to the kitchen, grabbed a jar, came back into the living room, and caught it, holding the jar against the glass. I asked Chelsea to hand me a magazine from the coffee table, then slid the magazine over the lip of the jar and brought it away from the window. Chelsea and I took a long look at the yellow jacket through the glass. I was captivated. I'd never been able to get such a good look at one before. Then Chelsea and I took the jar outside and let the wasp go.

My time in the monastery was still many years off. But I'd been granted a sudden enlightenment into what I later came to know as the first order of the *Way: Be as if one with all life.*

I was still alive then. At the moment I released the wasp, I was finally able to cry. I cherish the memory of that moment I shared with my sister. Unfortunately, in remembrance I may shed no such tears—as this corpse I've become can no longer produce them.

The Aspirant who has achieved *satori* now dons the robes of the Disciple and the Master inducts the student to the next level of study with three gifts of acknowledgment:

A tea ceremony to honor his *satori*.

A parchment reading as follows:

Te Four Noble Truths

1. All Life is Suffering.
2. All Suffering is caused by Selfishness.
3. All Selfishness can be overcome.
4. The Eightfold Path overcomes all.

The Eightfold Path

Right Understanding
Right Purpose

Right Speech
Right Conduct
Right Livelihood
Right Effort
Right Alertness
Right Concentration

Lastly, the Master presents his Disciple with a wooden stake, fashioned by him for this purpose, with the pointed end directed toward his own heart. The Disciple grasps the handle firmly with his dominant hand, involuntarily clutching it so forcefully (some say with the entirety of his being) that an imprint of his grip remains forever upon the wood.

This moment signifies the Disciple's departure from the direct path of Zen, the Artless Art, and his arrival on the path of Zen in the Art of Slaying Vampires (a departure paralleled in the reception of the Zen painter's brush, the Zen archer's bow, and the Zen swordsman's blade).

Known as the Stake of Atonement, once given, this weapon shall never leave the Disciple's possession. The Disciple reveres and will seek to become one with the Stake, knowing mastery over it shall one day become a matter of life and death.

Slaying vampires predates the introduction of the Stake, before which there was no Art to slaying vampires. Still, ways were found to kill them. Before detailing the Disciple's training, some history will be useful.

As far back as twenty-five centuries, during the lifetime of the Buddha, then still known as Prince Gautama, there were records of "those aligned with the power of darkness that feed on the *prana* (lifeforce) of the living." The action prescribed once such a creature had been discovered was to encircle the beast's lair in a ring of fire for seven days and nights. Fire is indeed capable of destroying a vampire, but it's difficult to control and would often be more dangerous to the village than the vampire itself. The next great leap in methodology seems to have developed during the eleventh century amid the border towns lining the shores of the Danube River in Rumania. Villagers tracked a vampire to its den using a white stallion that had never stumbled or been put to stud, then proceeded to nail the sleeping vampire down in its coffin with steel spikes, thereby preventing it from rising again to feed. This method would only have worked with fledgling vampires taken by surprise and unable to work the nails loose, who'd go insane with starvation and commit suicide by means of spontaneous combustion. Theoretically, a vampire thus entombed could remain so today, although no such instances have yet been uncovered.

This practice spread widely, becoming so prevalent that for a time in certain regions the remains of *all* deceased were nailed into their coffins preceding burial, as a precautionary measure.

I doubt many vampires met their demise in this fashion. There's no place more hazardous to a hunter than the lair of his prey, doubly so if that prey is a vampire.

It was not until the late thirteenth Century, when Bulgaria was nearly overrun with vampires, that the existing schools of Zen became involved. And their involvement unearthed a major dilemma, for the Masters had always considered the vampire to be a natural predator of Man, and yet here was a creature that subdued unnaturally the developmental progress of an individual's lifeforce. True, they were fair predators, as death itself is natural to Man, and many men were simply killed. Under what heading though, should they list these unearthly transformations that are not death and so blatantly arrest spiritual growth?

Finding themselves up against a new spiritual wall, they began a worldwide meditation, seeking understanding and guidance. After twelve years, a Tibetan hermit descended from his mountain dwelling to a monastery, proclaiming, *"Vampires who prey on* prana *chance encountering* prana *which preys on Vampires."*

This revelation created numerous divisions among Zen sects. Some, holding fast to their dictum *Be as if one with all life,* saw the call to war as a form of Zen genocide. Others heard the call and prepared themselves accordingly: throngs of Zen warriors left their monasteries in search of vampires.

By now vampire hordes had spread to India and China. Successful as trackers yet too easily dispatched by the unexpected prowess of the enemy, the warriors fell. Those who escaped alive and unturned delivered horrific accounts of savagery and were completely disheartened.

Clearly, some new Art of War needed to be developed to meet this dire threat.

Exact historical detail surrounding the founding of the sect was never properly recorded. The following has been passed on through oral tradition.

The Master of Masters, at one time an ascetic and student of the *Way,* lived a solitary life wandering in the East. One evening, he witnessed with horror a vampire as it drained a man in the streets of holy Tibet, and fell into a near cataleptic state for several weeks. When he recovered, he renounced asceticism and sought out the Zen sect waging war against vampires.

He found them weaponless and despondent after countless failed campaigns. Conflict by conflict his brethren fell. The Master himself nearly perished at least half a dozen times. Finally, he left them, to wander and seek guidance from the earth. Remembering how Prince Gautama achieved enlightenment after meditating seven days beneath a Bodhi tree, he searched for a Bodhi tree and found none. Exhausted and without food, unable to journey farther, he settled into meditation in a great clearing.

Some say he sat for a few days; others, a few weeks. The sun and moon rose and fell; rains came and went; winds stirred his hair. His bodily fluids issued from his form, seeping into the ground.

A seed germinated in the soil before him. Time passed; a slim shoot forced its way up through the soil, ending in a lush bud. Unaware, the Master continued sitting in stillness, his devotion unshaken, struggling to find a solution. Overnight, the bud became a sapling. Joined to the Master's lifepulse, the sapling strove to grow to fruition, its roots grasping the fertile soil, breaking the surface of the ground and encircling the Master.

One morning, he felt a shadow that should not be there fall across his face. He opened his eyes to behold a towering tree.

An Aspen.

In a flash he was at one with the tree, and understood the true meaning of sacrifice. Taking the knife from his belt, he carved twelve wooden stakes from the trunk: the Twelve Chaste Stakes of Atonement. Their existence has never been proven.

Soon the Master was joined by the first Aspirants of the Art of Slaying Vampires, finally in possession of the weapon they required—and Masters ever since have used aspen wood to make their Disciples' stakes.

———

TRAINING BEGINS at dawn the day after the Disciple receives his weapon. The Disciple arrives, bows to his Master, and enters into meditation and recitation of the Eightfold Path. Then the first lesson begins.

The Master instructs the student to pay strict attention to his every move, then walks in circles around the Disciple, saying, "This is a matter of life and death."

The circling continues, the Master sometimes swinging or thrusting his hands in seemingly sporadic bursts at the Disciple's head or torso, sometimes stepping toward or away from him erratically. To the Disciple, the Master appears to be drawing patterns in the air. The Master continues bobbing, weaving, and circling the student until satisfied he's explored and defined all the aspects of the student's perimeter. The Disciple may experience mild nausea during this initial experience.

"This is the killing ground," the Master says. "You must release yourself from the confines of your body and shift your six senses into this new circumference. Draw your weapon!"

The Disciple pulls the Stake from his robe, instinctively grasping it with the same grip with which he first received it. This is his true grip, the only hold that can prevent the Stake from ever being torn from his hand.

The Master now instructs the Disciple to thrust the Stake.

"Where?" the Disciple asks. "At what?"

"Go!" the Master commands.

The Disciple turns, spearing the Stake into empty air without thinking—then halts, realizing what he's just done.

"Again!" demands the Master.

The Disciple spends a moment in contemplation, then thrusts at the air again.

"You have missed," chides the Master. "You are dead."

The student feels the shadow of truth brush him.

"Now you have experienced both the hit and the miss," the Master explains, "and you are sure to recognize the difference in the future. Practice your thrusts for the remainder of the day. Strike only where compelled to strike. Learn the killing ground. Take no meals today. I'll return at dusk."

The Master leaves.

The bewildered Disciple takes his third swing with some trepidation, his fourth with excitement, his fifth with humility. And so the day proceeds. The Disciple tires, often losing his concentration or balance. Still he perseveres, determined not to disappoint his Master.

For the next few weeks the Disciple struggles to acquaint himself with each potential thrust within the killing ground. If he is part of a community of Disciples, he may spend mealtimes comparing his progress with his fellows', sometimes hearing horror stories about Aspirants who faltered toward the end of the training. Rumor has it the final exam's a killer.

The Master permits the Disciple to ask one question per day, at the conclusion of his evening meditation.

"What does it take to know the killing ground?" he asks.

"Superior focus," the Master answers.

Depending on how fluid his movements become, the

soreness in every muscle begins to subside by the third or fourth week. Sometimes the Disciple may demonstrate a thrust he's particularly comfortable with, certain he's made great progress.

"You are dead," the Master informs him. "This hit was not true. You made it because your body feels secure doing so. Forget your body. Perceive through the killing ground."

That night, the Disciple is unable to sleep. He plays the scenario repeatedly in his head. His follow-through on that last hit felt correct. He's sure he'd made it correctly.

The next day he's about to make the same thrust, confident his movement is true. The Master intervenes.

"You are attempting to cheat me; I won't tolerate it. You have mastered this simple thrust and are allowing your body to choose it for you. Open your senses to the killing ground. Wait for the precise moment to strike. *Let the strike deliver itself.*"

The chastened Disciple stands ready.

"Close your eyes!" the Master yells.

His eyes close.

"Allow the strike to deliver itself."

The Disciple waits. Minutes pass. He hears only his own breathing. His thoughts race; he ignores them.

A loud burst slices through the silence—the Master clapping his hands.

"Drop away from your body!"

The Disciple blurs forward in a perfect thrusting motion.

The Master bows to the truth of the thrust.

"That strike was not made within your body. It was sensed through the killing ground."

"Where does the strike come from?"

The Master smiles. He covers his abdomen with an open

hand, then points to the center of his forehead, then holds his palm outward to the Disciple: a simple, fluid series of gestures.

The Disciple bows low.

The Master chuckles.

Several weeks later the Disciple is striking more and more frequently at the compulsion of the killing ground. His outward appearance reflects this to the enlightened eye. He walks confidently, rarely speaks of his progress to his fellows, spends almost every waking hour in the practice room.

"How shall I best occupy my time when not practicing?" he asks the Master.

"Go through each strike you've learned step by step in your mind. Again and yet again."

Thereafter, the Disciple will always be striking his Stake through his opponent's heart, whether shaving in the morning before the mirror, raising food to his lips, or watering plants in the garden, thus magnifying his physical thrusting ability in the training sessions. Rarely does he fail to strike truthfully. Still he knows it isn't enough.

"How can I yet improve my ability to strike?" he asks the Master.

"Go through every strike posture while at your deepest level of meditation. Focus your entire being in each thrust, as though it were occurring one muscle at a time. Be one with that muscle and only that muscle, until it is time to activate the next muscle. Witness the transition fully. Do not seek me out until you have achieved this, or I shall cast you from the Art forever."

Yearning to achieve this experience, the Disciple divides his day into three segments—physical training, meditation, and daily existence—spending the third only on the basic necessities of sleeping, eating, and bathing, the latter two in intense mental rehearsal.

CHELSEA SUFFERED several nervous breakdowns while we were living with our cousins in New Mexico. She withdrew from the world in some unspoken pain she couldn't share with me. Finally, she was taken away to an institution.

I visited her often. She lay in her room all day, lost in her own world, apparently not knowing who she was, where she was, or who I was.

Eventually, I couldn't handle it anymore. I was screwed up, too. One day I sat on her bed, holding her hand as long as I could, and left.

My sister was gone. I was alone.

Several bleak months later, I received a scholarship from a prestigious university in New York City. I waved goodbye to my cousins and hitchhiked back to the East Coast.

The scholarship provided me with a small stipend, barely enough for food and a fourth of the rent for the studio apartment I shared with three other students.

I flung myself into my studies, poring through centuries of literary masters, attending lectures and films, drowning myself in my coursework and drinking myself into forgetfulness at East Village dives for nearly four years, looking for escape. One day melted into the next.

During my senior year, I finally took the required course in world religion.

"Zen is a Japanese form of Buddhism in which enlightenment is reached through meditation, contemplation, and intuition, according to Webster's New Riverside Dictionary," explained the professor. "Does anyone in class today meditate regularly?"

A young woman in the back raised her hand.

"Yes, Deirdre. What form of meditation do you practice?"

"Mantra," she said.

"Would you mind demonstrating?"

Deirdre rose, made her way to the head of the class, and in one graceful movement assumed the lotus position atop the professor's desk and almost immediately fell into a trance-like state.

Pleased, the professor smiled and continued lecturing. Deirdre sat, eyes closed, quietly repeating words I couldn't decipher, a lithe and powerful dark-haired vision radiating calm. I glanced around, noting several other students, female as well as male, were similarly attracted. I was either the bravest or merely the fastest to approach her at the end of class and invite her out for coffee.

We'd hardly begun sipping when I asked if she was dating anyone.

"Nothing serious," she said. "Why do you think I have so much time to meditate?"

We both laughed. I felt comfortable enough to tell her about my parents' death and my sister's subsequent condition. I sensed a bond with Deirdre, as if I'd known and loved her—it was that strong—in some other time, some other place. I think she felt it, too, though neither of us said anything. We must have gone through four pots of coffee before bidding each other good night.

It was a Thursday. Our next class wasn't until Tuesday. I spent the days until then unaccountably bereft, longing to see her again. Yes, I wanted her. But there was something deeper than sex at work. Deirdre made me feel alive, for the first time in years.

We began seeing each other regularly after class. My pain subsided when I was with her. The rest of the time, my thoughts were always of her, distracting me at lectures, rendering me oblivious in conversations, although no one took me to task. I had no friends, and no one minded enough to do so.

One evening Deirdre introduced me to her suitemate at her dormitory, blushing when Kirsten excitedly blurted out that Deirdre talked about me all the time. I thrilled at Kirsten's indiscretion. The three of us chatted for a few hours, sitting on Deirdre's bed (a fact that intoxicated me). Finally, Kirsten excused herself with an overdramatic yawn.

That night, Deirdre and I made love for the first time, with an erotic familiarity as if we'd always been lovers. Twisted together, skin against skin, we revealed ourselves to each other, soul to soul.

A few weeks later, I moved (illegally) into her dorm room. From then on, we spent every moment we could together, seeing films, going to plays, taking all the same courses our final semester. During lectures I took notes while she listened intently, a system that helped greatly with exams.

She cajoled me into meditating with her, promising it would enrich our relationship not only spiritually but sexually. The latter was incentive enough, though I found it hard to imagine our sex life could get any better. Still, my participation at first was less than wholehearted.

"Come on," she'd chide. "Cross those legs."

"But it hurts," I'd complain.

She'd smile and suggest another way.

"That's sort of it. Now the chant: *Om mani padme hum*."

This is the Indian Mantra of Compassion, a phrase she said could transform my six negative manifestations—pride, jealousy, desire, ignorance, greed, and anger—into the six transcendental actions of the heart of the enlightened mind —generosity, harmonious conduct, endurance, enthusiasm, concentration, and insight.

Whatever, I thought.

We'd chant quietly together until I could no longer bear the pain of the lotus position. Then I'd sit watching her in the soft glow of the candle she'd lit to help me focus my attention. Deirdre needed no such aid. She could meditate for hours, her eyes open, rarely blinking, as if she were looking into some limitless expanse beyond the dorm room.

Once her mother called from Tucson and I couldn't bring her out of it to answer the phone. Later she admitted she'd heard me talking, but what she was doing was much more important, a matter of life and death.

I was getting nothing from chanting, and felt I must be doing it wrong. If anything, I disbelieved in the benefits altogether. Our sex life certainly hadn't changed.

I suggested giving up on meditating.

"Just use the chanting to clear everything out of your head," she responded. "Say it whenever a random thought enters your mind. Then say it again. Let it chase the thoughts right out of Dodge. That might be the best way for you. Don't worry about where I am. Just be where you are."

She left me alone and went down to the corner grocery.

I sat on the edge of the bed and said the mantra once. Suddenly tears started flowing in torrents. There was no sadness I could put a finger on—yet there I sat crying hysterically.

She found me like that when she returned. Saying nothing, she laid me back on the bed and started massaging my shoulders. Deirdre had a way of being acutely aware of my thoughts and emotions whenever she gave me massages (and sometimes during sex), nearly clairvoyant.

"It's Chelsea," she said. "You feel you've wronged your sister."

"I left her all alone in that place!"

She brought my face close to hers, tears welling in her own eyes.

"What else could you have done?" she whispered.

"I don't know. Something. Anything."

"You had no other choice, darling. Just like your parents didn't choose to leave the two of you. Things happen as part of our karmic plan. You did what you had to do."

"Don't ever leave me."

"I'm not going anywhere, silly. But take a look at this!"

She pulled out a folded piece of gray stationary she'd taken from the grocer's window, for my teary-eyed inspection—

1 BEDROOM APARTMENT DOWNTOWN.
PERFECT FOR COUPLE AND ACCESS TO
ALL SUBWAYS. CALL

—with the telephone number.

"We'll go tomorrow," she said, stroking my hair. "We'll see this place, love it, move right in, and be happy there. Okay?"

"Okay."

We signed a year's lease within forty-five minutes of seeing it, a top floor of a townhouse off Avenue A. The rent was a bit beyond our means, but the oversized antique bathtub, beamed ceilings, and mosaic hardwood floors made it impossible to pass up.

Kirsten was at home in Wichita or someplace, with a serious flu. We left her a note saying we'd call when we got a phone, and moved in all our stuff that evening, camping out in the living room without electricity, water, heat, or even outside light. The windows in all the rooms were boarded up, empty apartments in the neighborhood being prone to broken glass. The downstairs apartments were vacant, in the final stages of renovation.

I went for groceries, and came back to find Deirdre deep in trance, beautiful as always, softly mouthing the mantra by candlelight. Standing in the doorway, holding my keys and the grocery bags, I wanted desperately to see what she was seeing, know what she knew, to share with her completely.

I didn't even take off my jacket. Leaving the bags on the floor, I sat down across from Deirdre, crossed my legs in the painful position, settled my gaze on the candle, and started to chant, "*Ommanipadmehum. Ommanipadmehum.*"

Slowly, my breathing coursed to the pain in my leg muscles. They stopped hurting. I began doing what she'd always told me to do, chasing my nervous, jumping thoughts from my head with the chant, acknowledging them as they kept coming and throwing them off. Finally, my head went silent except for the mantra. Warmth streamed out of my hands. A ball of fire sat just beneath my stomach.

An image floated into my mind, getting clearer, refusing to be chased away: Deirdre and I seated across from each other on a beach. We were speaking, but there were no words coming out of our mouths. Whenever I tried to speak this thick black smoke poured from my lips and nostrils.

Each time it happened she took a deep breath and inhaled the smoke into her lungs. Her reply came in the form of dazzling white light pouring out from her mouth. I breathed it in. My next words were black smoke again, and again she replied with white light. We breathed in time like that for what seemed an eternity and I saw the black smoke I was speaking becoming lighter and lighter shades of gray. *I love you,* I was trying to say to her with the smoke. *I love you, too,* she kept replying. Then with one final labored gasp, I choked out what looked like a thick chunk of black coal. After that we sat breathing together in cycle, my breath clear and flowing easily, and I thought, *she's cleaning me, my God, I feel like she's cleaning my soul!*

I took a deep, heaving breath as the vision ended. My whole body tingled. I opened my eyes and saw my love still deep in trance, across from me in the candlelight.

I began sobbing. She opened her eyes and smiled.

"You were really in that time. I can see it. Sometimes it takes a while, but I knew you would finally get it right. I'm so proud of you."

We skipped classes the next day and set to work vacuuming, sanding, and painting. We scrubbed grime from the bathtub, teasingly anticipating using it as soon as possible. The deliverymen arrived, complaining about the five-floor walk-up as they brought in our new bed and kitchen set.

That afternoon the electric came on.

The next day we had running water.

"We have to get those boards off the windows and let some light in," Deirdre said.

"I'll see to it, tomorrow," I promised. "Is the telephone working yet?"

"Who cares?" she said. "I don't need to speak to anyone but you. You know that, don't you?"

That night I insisted we eat out to celebrate our hard work, even though we couldn't afford it.

"To the apartment," she said, raising her wineglass.

"To you," I insisted. "I love you so much."

We left the restaurant very satisfied, promising ourselves we'd dine there again. Arm in arm, we walked happily beneath a high lover's moon. Deirdre tickled me under my jacket.

"Don't forget, you promised to take the boards off the windows," she said as we turned up an alley toward Houston Street and three creatures out of nightmare emerged from the shadows.

5

Inevitably, the training evolves beyond the theoretical, and the Disciple must endeavor to slay his foe.

"The killing ground is mine," proclaims the Disciple.

"Is it so?" replies the Master.

"It is so."

Thus begins the rite of passage known as the Blackened Gate. The Disciple has twenty-four hours in which to meditate, pray, practice, or prepare himself in any way he chooses. No other Disciple or Master (except infirmary workers) attends to normal daily duties during this sacred period. All spend their time in meditations prescribed to siphon distraction from their colleague, whose failure to traverse the Blackened Gate falls on his Master, his monastery, and the entire Ministry. No member of the community may speak to the Disciple or hinder him in any way. All physical contact is forbidden.

The Disciple moves about as though he were the sole member of the community. He meditates on the trial to come, does sensory deprivation exercises, and observes the

Masters who sit within their zendos praying for his success. Perhaps he enters the restricted chamber where *The Book of Life and Death* is kept—to read the success and failure records regarding this final exam—and finds a solemn comment scribbled within the margins, repeated beside far too many names, *Strove too soon to pass the Blackened Gate*.

He notes the empty space where his name will appear.

He reaches to feel the course texture of the weapon hanging by his side, certain the Stake will see him through.

At the twenty-fourth sounding of the bell he has already arrived at the prescribed chamber, and stands before a gathering of Masters, some known and others foreign to his zendo. A holy mantra is spoken (which may not be recorded) and the test shall begin.

Four Masters strain to remove a harsh stone slab to uncover the entrance to a subterranean chamber. The Master nods to the Disciple, who nods back.

The Disciple is lowered into the pit. His eyes dilate for a momentary glimpse of the area—a putrid cave some thirty feet square—as the slab is replaced. Then all is darkness.

He shifts his position immediately, controlling his breath as he draws the Stake.

In the darkness opposite, a panel opens and closes with the sound of scraping stone. Something has entered. A faint keening noise begins, ramps up. An acrid smell assaults the Disciple.

He grips his weapon tightly, circles left, expanding his senses outward.

A movement to his left; he strikes at empty air.

Impossible, he thinks. *Something was there!*

It lashes from the blackness, tears flesh from the Disciple's chest. He reels backward. To consider his wound would be fatal. Instead, he circles again, Stake held low, poised to strike.

Again the slashing fist, to his forehead. He ignores the blood coursing around his left eye, down his face. The keening continues in the blackness, the scent maddening his nostrils.

The starving vampire lunges from behind, claws extended, fangs eager to feed. The Disciple experiences a rapturous instant of nothingness, surrendering to the killing ground in a muscle-wrenching spin and driving the Stake into the vampire's heart.

Stones grate above him. Light pours in.

A Slayer has traversed the Blackened Gate.

IT SEEMED a long way down to the pavement. My throat was torn. I was dying.

My life flashed before me, from the day I was born through my parents' deaths, saying goodbye to my sister, falling in love with Deirdre, and turning in to this alley. Somehow, I wasn't frightened. A soft, fragrant breeze stirred in the blackness, increasing by degrees into a gale and building in force to hurricane velocity, sweeping me up and out of my body into a dark tunnel, tearing me free of this world with each twist and turn. A faint gleam of light appeared ahead, increasing as I moved. Joy pervaded me, propelling me onward. I wanted to become one with the radiance. I approached the outer edge of the tunnel.

Suddenly a row of steel bars crashed down, blocking the way. I slammed hard against them, unable to continue to the light.

I hung suspended, howling with frustration. Some primal force within me, frantically seeking an alternate escape route from my body, reversed my direction, throttling me back down the dark tunnel. My thoughts raced, *get out, escape my body, get out before it's too late!*

Somehow I found another exit, seemingly through my navel, my essence exploding from my physical body. For a moment, I was free, an ethereal form in the alley. My heart leapt.

Something bit my neck and my wrists, violently jarring me to a halt just beyond my body, grappling me and reeling me backward, downward, and inward, sealing me again in my flesh.

I still don't know whether these were delusions produced by my dying physical body or images of my death and turning. Whichever, my stomach was still burning when I woke on the ground and saw Deirdre's ravaged body lying across from me, the words KILL TO LIVE! scrawled in blood across the brick wall behind her.

I crawled to her, held her to me, tried to breathe into her lungs, praying she wasn't really dead.

The burning in my stomach grew worse. I had to seek help. Somehow I got up, telling myself this couldn't be happening as I staggered toward Houston Street, stumbling and retching and covered with blood, crying out to passersby, begging them to come to our aid, not understanding that there was nothing anyone could do to help either of us.

Everyone ignored me. Desperate, I threw myself in front of an oncoming car. It sent me sprawling twenty-or-so feet. That finally drew a crowd, who were more than a little startled when I stood up. As more and more people gathered around to gawk at this student who was more than likely speeding on drugs, I took a long look at them. A soft glow flowed freely about their faces and hands—grotesque, hideous, monstrous.

"Get away from me!" I screamed.

Sirens blared in the distance, growing louder as they neared. Someone moved toward me, his blood pumping violently through the opaque veins of his face, his outstretched hand, accompanied by that weird glow. I was terrified and, although I didn't understand it yet, blood-starved. Confused, in pain, I fled.

In record time, I found myself several blocks away. Seeing a police box, I stopped running. I think I tore the cover off the hinges. I hit the button and heard a female voice.

"911 what's your emergency?"

"Dead, she's dead—they butchered her!" I shouted, and crumpled in a heap at the base of the box.

"Sir, please slow down and tell me what's happening."

"I don't know what the fuck's happening!"

I dropped the phone as the burning flared again in my stomach, the pain flattening me on the pavement. Through the agony I sensed dawn approaching—and I was immediately terrified. I mean, some raw, primal survival instinct just reached out and got me on my feet and sent me running for refuge—like the devil himself was chasing me—hell-bent to rip me apart again.

6

After successfully traversing the Blackened Gate, the new Slayer dons the robes of the Initiate. His success bodes well for the Ministry, and word spreads quickly from monastery to monastery on its global networks.

Critically wounded, successfully achieved, the Master inscribes alongside the Initiate's name in *The Book of Life and Death*.

The remains of the slain vampire (little more than ashes and bits of bone), are intermingled with the sacred herbs chaparral, Echinacea, garlic, and St. John's wort, to prevent future corruptive influence, the mixture then ground into a fine powder to make it earth-friendly. This powder is divided into unequal portions and delivered to agents for worldwide disposal, thereby concealing the monastery of origin. (The distinctive scent of the defeated vampire's ashes also sends an unmistakable warning to others of its kind. It really wigs them out.)

Monastery life resumes as normal the next day. The Master meditates at his wounded Disciple's bedside in the infirmary, concerned only with his swift recovery, knowing the true road to rejuvenation lies not in the salves applied to his wounds, but from correct energy channeled through the core of his *prana*. When fevered spasms indicate lack of focus, the Master helps channel this *pranic* energy. He will not leave the bedside until either the Disciple has regained the strength of will to heal himself or one of them has died. Such is the devotion between Master and Disciple.

I WOKE at sunset in our dark apartment—where else could I have gone?—where I'd collapsed unconscious on the new bed Deirdre and I would never share, grateful for the boarded-over windows. Deirdre's favorite jeans lay on the floor, amid a pile of clothing to be laundered. Madness, to think we'd left here filled with laughter and *life* scant hours ago.

I looked in the bathroom mirror. My face was bloated, my skin unnaturally pale. The irises in my eyes were huge, alarmingly dark, the whites nearly nonexistent. But the true horrors were my eyeteeth—sharp, elongated, not teeth but fangs.

A vampire's reflection.

Was it possible? I was cold. I felt hollowed out. At the same time, my guts were on fire. I knew in my depths I needed blood. My whole being cried out for it. I'd seen it flowing in the people on the street. I could smell what little remained inside me, *feel* how it would taste. Hunger for it seized me in spasms.

I crumpled in agony on the living room floor, vomiting

the remains of last night's dinner, undigested and tinged with blood, inwardly screaming, *Please! Let me die!*

The pain dwindled to a tolerable level where I could at least stand. I looked around me with new vision. Clearer. Richer. All my senses were heightened. I could smell and hear mice scampering behind the walls, distinguish myriad individual sounds of the bustling city outside the boarded-up windows. The mirror revealed the disgusting state of my clothes. I stripped them off, drew myself a bath, and scrubbed away the filth.

My body was changed, the skin tighter, corpse-like, cold to the touch despite the steaming bathwater. My nails were tough and dangerously sharp; blood trickled from several self-inflicted cuts on my arms. My canine teeth seemed to overrun my mouth, painfully puncturing my tongue if I wasn't careful.

As vile fluids drained in the tub, I went into the bedroom, found a carton containing some of my clothing, and managed to dress myself. Then I worked up the courage to look at myself again in the mirror, hoping against hope my reflection would have returned to normal. It hadn't. I convinced myself it was still me staring back, not some monster, and took a good, long look.

Trauma had chiseled distress marks in my stark, pallid features. My eyes were so dilated they seemed owlish. My canine teeth were enormous, and sharp. There was no wound in my neck where it had been torn.

Pain seized me again, forcing me to my knees. White-hot fire filled my veins. If I wanted to stay alive, I'd have to go out and kill—*soon*. I told myself to hold on, just a moment longer. The moments passed. The pain didn't.

I *would not* let myself become a killer. And somehow I

managed to remain in the apartment until finally sleep came again as the sun rose outside.

I woke the next evening determined to end the pain and join Deirdre wherever she had flown. The first vampire I would slay would be myself. If I was going to be dead, at least I'd control how and when.

It wasn't the first time in my life I thought about killing myself; it just made more sense now. I could never again touch another human being, for fear of losing control. That must never be allowed to happen.

I took my straight razor from the medicine cabinet and turned on the bath, psyching myself up by staring at my reflection in the mirror. I got in the tub and laid the razor on the soap dish. The hot water was soothing; I felt almost human, almost alive again. I was ready. I'd lie there, think of Deirdre, wait for the hunger pains, and slice. Whatever came after was sure to be better than this.

The pain came. I sliced deep, screaming while I did it. Again and again, until long, deep gashes stretched from my palms to the middle of my forearms. I closed my eyes, brought my arms under the steaming water, and waited, whispering, "Deirdre."

Nothing happened. I opened my eyes. The water was clear. I raised my arms. Through the gashes I saw my veins, my arm muscles, bits of bone. No blood flowed.

The pain hit me hard again. I sliced and sliced, always with the same results. Finally, I stopped slicing and lay in the cold water as wave after wave of pain seized my body. And damned if the cuts didn't begin to mend themselves; within the hour, only pale scars remained.

I got out of the tub, dressed, and went up to the roof, and learned the hard way that vampire bones can break and even splinter, and when the *un*dead are injured, their hunger pains increase exponentially. After several hours at the foot of the fire escape in the alley behind the building, I pulled myself with my hands up the escape ladder, back to the roof, and somehow crawled down to the apartment, grateful that the apartments below weren't rented yet.

I spent the remaining hours until sunrise in dizzying pain as my bones slowly knitted themselves together until they were good as new.

Killing myself was going to be a lot harder than I'd thought.

The next night, I considered other possibilities. Dismemberment was out of the question, even if I could figure out a way to manage it. Logistics similarly ruled out hanging—I pictured myself dangling, endlessly choking with no way to get down—as well as staking myself in the chest.

Finally, I settled on exposing myself to the sun. But standing on the roof with the sun rising, I lost my nerve. Some unnatural survival instinct was too great to overcome.

What was happening? It was inexplicable I could still have such an irrational fear. I wanted death. The sun remained an alternative I'd have to deal with if all else failed.

The only thing left was starvation, the course I'd already been unmindfully following. I had no idea how long death by blood deprivation might take. And how would I survive the hunger pains? Somehow willpower, the determination not to kill another human being, had seen me through the past few days. But it was getting harder and harder. I was terrified bloodlust would conquer me and send me ravening.

I missed Deirdre. I longed to see her again.

And suddenly it was as if I could hear her voice telling me to empty myself.

"Use the mantra."

The chant sprang into my head: *Om mani padme hum. Om mani padme hum.*

Each night the pain returned, and each night it found me deep in meditation, dreading its arrival but also resigned. Somehow I managed to endure wave after wave of agony with increasing resilience, reciting the mantra. At moments the pain would ebb and cease, then crash back. I kept chanting.

Om mani padme hum. Om mani padme hum.

Each night when I rose from sleep, I looked at the mirror to see the effects of my starvation. The lines in my face were growing deeper; as the end of the month neared, my skull was clearly visible beneath the skin. Now I welcomed the pain, enduring each spasm as a prelude to release.

Then came the night the final drops of blood dwindled to dust inside me.

Though, when they were gone, I tell you I found not the expected release I had longed for—but an all-pervading landscape of emptiness—a desert of *nothingness* stretching out to infinite ends within my perception.

It was there on those sands that I rested.

7

I nitiate awaken, your *prana* has mended, a sick world now beckons for you to rise up and offer your Art. And to this calling, if in any way he can respond then he shall overcome his *un*natural wounds and open up his eyes to find The Master who has prayed so diligently for his recovery. The imminent danger passed; the Master's heart may rejoice in this triumph, for he has once more traversed the Blackened Gate vicariously through the proper guidance of his student.

The Chinese have a fable that accords well with this. It seems that somewhere deep within the earth's bowels there dwells the Horrid Blue Dragon. It is said that when a person suffers an affliction that carries him near to the brink of death, that to affect his own return to life he must first descend to face this Blue Dragon. The way is perilous, and the Dragon itself is said to be boundless there within its realm. Its power is a secret knowledge of the karma of all men and women. Within the mouth of the Blue Dragon there rests a silver key. A dying man must find some way to retrieve this key from the Dragon's mouth, or he can never return to consciousness. It has been suggested that those patients who lie within comas for years have either lost their way or are afraid to confront The Blue. A Man may face similar trials several times during the natural course of his life, and may, in time, befriend the Dragon, depending on how many keys he endeavors to seek.

Before long, the wounded student is removed from the sick room and has taken up minor duties about the monastery; perhaps he will be made the attendant responsible for Feeding the Hungry Ghosts; the burning of a special incense at a prescribed shrine, the smoke of which is regarded as a source of nourishment for restless ancestral spirits; or tending the bells that sound throughout the daily cycle of a monastery, alerting the Disciples to prayer times, meal times, and meditation periods—as well as the arrival, departure, or death of their fellows.

As he passes his colleagues within the monastery, both Aspirants and Disciples alike, he hears whispering of praise and veneration for his ascension. At mealtimes they'll hawk about and badger him with questions regarding the encounter, all beneath the watchful eyes of the Masters. His descriptions will be useless to them, of course. For nothing he would advise could offer them any defense against their own future trials. He tells them, "What you bring in with you is your Stake, nothing more, nothing less. Know the killing ground and you'll make it through."

And if prodded enough, perhaps he will show them his wounds.

NOTHINGNESS ... is like a grand *satori*. It's like spending your whole life in a state of natural blindness, then suddenly gaining the power of sight, so intense and captivating for those first few moments of unknown sensation that you are consumed within it to the point where you lose your conscious awareness of self. It was barren, desolate, empty, and I was floating there within it. I ceased to be aware of my own existence. The voice that was, until that time, my ever-shifting constant inner dialogue simply stopped. And the only hint of an association that I can place upon the experience to give it any form of substantiality within my own mind, then or now, was the profoundly contrasting intrusion to that interminable nothingness made by the reemergence of myself. Myself-ness. I came back to my body again. Or perhaps I should say, I came back to a conscious *awareness* of my body.

Where moments, perhaps centuries, before there had been nothingness, and prior to the nothingness there had been several fleeting drops of blood ... now some new thing was hot and struggling to emerge from the pit of my stomach ...

And then *it* sprang from the very core of my being. Wave after wave of energy burst through my hollow husk, shocking me back to awareness. An empowering, revitalizing, sensual and luminescent energy. *It* streamed and surged within the corpse that I'd become. It *filled* me.

I just sat there, basking in it, shuddering at times, letting it have its way with me. It fed me, changed me ... *saved* me.

I was revitalized, free of pain, knowing it wouldn't return as long as this precious new nourishment that wasn't blood coursed through my system.

I did somersaults throughout the apartment, laughing myself silly, exploding with delight.

But what did it mean and why had it happened and for how long would it continue like this? I stopped to consider, suddenly sobering. And was I still a vampire, a potential killer? Was I free of the need for blood? Or would the pains return again? What might happen now, were I to encounter a human being?

My body was unchanged, although my face already displayed signs of rejuvenation. And so began a new series of experiments I conducted upon myself. I opened a wound on my hand with a kitchen knife; it healed to a thin scar in moments—an acceleration of the normal healing process with no blood involved. I repeated the action several times with the same results.

My senses had been strongly augmented after death; without the distracting hunger pains, I was able to gauge them better.

I didn't need to turn on the lights to see clearly in the pitch-black apartment (I never did un-board those windows, my love). If anything, the electric light was almost painful, although in it I was able to discern light in ways formerly imperceptible—as near constant fluidity. I could observe an insect's movements at the opposite end of the apartment. I heard the new tenants in the building: two women on the second floor and an older man with a dog and two cats on the first. (The fourth-floor apartment remained unoccupied.)

The refrigerator yielded several month-old specimens to assure me both my powers of smell and taste had been intensified. And my fingertips were overly sensitized to the point where touching anything at all could fill me with long moments of distraction over newly discovered textures. It was only upon touching myself that the joys of discovery would begin to wane as my self-fascination always led itself back into the awareness of my deathlike condition—which in turn could breed entire catalogs of self-revulsion.

The question was, would the hunger return? Vitality flowed through me but fear of the pain loomed at the edge of my mind. What might happen if I encountered a human being?

In any case, I'd continue chanting.

SEVERAL NIGHTS PASSED and the vitality remained. I couldn't remain confined in the apartment indefinitely. No matter how much peace and serenity I felt, did I dare risk going outside where there were living, breathing people capable of bleeding?

There was only one way to find out.

The boards with which I had previously sealed myself in, which I'd thought so secure, tore free with alarming ease.

I descended the five flights of stairs mentally repeating the mantra, continuing as I stepped through the front door into the warm flow of human traffic. My vampire sight took in every passing man, woman, and child. No one was alarmed by my presence and, despite the sound of blood coursing through their bodies, I had not the least desire to feed on any of them.

8

The Initiate, restored to health after proving himself in mortal combat, still has much to learn. Full mastery may take decades to achieve.

He has several options.

He may return to civilian life and serve as *eyes* for the Ministry. In such cases, the Ministry creates a proper history and identity for the Initiate, securing him employment and whatever else he needs in this new life.

The Initiate who feels no compulsion to continue training nor wish to rejoin civilian life may become a Rogue Vampire Slayer, moving from city to city, gaining mastery or encountering his demise. The Ministry attempts to chart his progress, but this is difficult. Unless a Rogue makes contact with a former Master or visits a local monastery in his travels, his deeds remain mostly unsung and unrecorded.

The majority of Initiates join the Ministry, availing themselves of the agency's vast body of knowledge, including numerous courses of instruction, known as the Vampire Sciences.

Whatever his choice, the Initiate remains a sentinel of the *Way*, dedicated to preserving Humanity.

——————

I WOULD LIVE, for how long I knew not since my sustenance came to me from sources unknown, and since unknown thus difficult to replenish. Animating my form in lieu of blood, as it were, the wellspring of the *Non*Vampire would remain shrouded in mystery.

I cast my attention then to worldly tasks and I discovered a horde of unopened mail jammed up in our mailbox thanks to those little pink change of address cards. No one had known where we'd moved except the US Postal Service, not even Kirsten, I realized. That was the reason I'd been left undisturbed. Deirdre had even left the telephone unlisted.

There was an overdue rent bill; thank goodness the landlord had been patient enough not to intrude upon my metamorphosis. Imagine! There were final notices on both our electric and water bills, though both past balances were little more than a few dollars as I had rarely used either. A postcard from Kirsten from Wichita that read, "Where the hell are you guys?" And several letters forwarded from either my original apartment or from the dormitory. One particular letter, written in her mother's handwriting had filled me with instant dread.

What did she know by now? Who had found Deirdre's murdered body in the alleyway? How could any police investigation proceed in regard to a slaying by vampires? And what about those devil butchers? Did they know that in me they had failed to finish what they'd begun? Could I have been implicated in the murder? Where had she been buried? How am I going to find all of these things out? And finally, after allowing these unanswerable questions time to run rampant, I remember thinking, *Thank God she need not have survived here as I did. God rest you, my love. I miss you ...*

I rummaged around the apartment until I located my checkbook. I still had enough money to cover the bills for a few months, what with considering I no longer needed to eat.

One letter was from the university proclaiming that my grades had been held back due to several overdue library fines. It made me laugh to think that indeed I was still considered a student and could, if I wished, still go back. Hell, I could've attended night classes if I'd wanted to.

And then a similar letter for Deirdre announced that her cumulative grade point average had dropped two points due to her failure to attend two final examinations; however, if she would please telephone the guidance department as soon as possible they'd see about correcting the matter. I almost wanted to ring them up myself right then in a moment of selfish outrage, just to find out how they might go about this correction of the matter.

Then there was only the letter her mother had written, and eventually I brought myself to open it. It had been written two days before she was killed—before *we* were killed. Her mother spoke of the neighbors who always inquired as to how Deirdre's studies were going, and she wanted to know if Deirdre was planning to be home for Winter recess or not? She mentioned that both Deirdre's father and sister had recently gotten over the flu. Then she made some vague inquiry as to "that young man you had mentioned on the telephone," apparently a reference to me. So, I assumed that her family didn't really know that I existed. Perhaps she hadn't been ready to disclose the depth of our relationship? Now she never could. Strange though, for some odd reason I wanted them to know who I was and what we had meant to each other. I created a fantasy in which they welcomed me into their home with open arms and held me as if their daughter and I had been married for years and then over steaming cups of hot chocolate we would while away the hours as they told me all about her childhood mishaps and in turn I related all of the courses and caresses that we'd shared. *Shit.*

"Om Mani Padme Hum. Om Mani Padme Hum."

DEIRDRE'S COSMETICS, through long hours of experimentation, were sufficient to dilute my stark pallid complexion, and both gloves and dark glasses enabled me to move around the city looking like nobody out of the ordinary. I could walk the streets for hours, just observing passers-by in all their living, breathing splendor.

The school library, which remained opened at all hours of the night, with its dimly lit entrance and secluded receptacles, provided me with a great deal of solace. I spent months on end devouring each volume I located that related, however remotely, to either vampirism or any affiliated occult research. It was nearly unbearable how little was actually known, at least as far as modern medicine was concerned, regarding my affliction. Only in one out of a thousand medical journals could I find any modern physician even willing to speculate that Vampirism *might* possibly exist or *could,* though it was highly unlikely, bear some hidden relationship to various blood disorders—such as anemia, a blood oxygen deficiency, or hemophilia, which can cause excessive bleeding—in which a crazed sufferer could have been attempting to replace their lost blood with the blood of another. Or consider the rare disfiguring disease called porphyria which can result in a drastic enlargement of both the teeth and jaw, accompanied by an odd phosphorescence to the hair and nails. This disease is often treated in modern medicine with injections of heme, an extract of the hemoglobin of the red blood cell. Those so afflicted in ancient times may have, either instinctively, or under the guidance of a physician of great foresight, ingested large amounts of blood to gain this strange curative property.

But none of these diseases could account for my captive reanimation, nor my heightened senses, nor my inhuman capacity to withstand so indefinite a time without nourishment. Dead ends.

So, what I was left with was merely a large body of folklore from which I derived several rather dubious facts regarding the causes and effects of the "curse" of the vampire.

For instance, I learned that supposedly a vampire shall not be able to cross, not by bridge nor by boat, any significant body of water. This I proceeded to prove false later that evening by commuting back and forth across the East River upon a Number Two subway and then proceeded to reinforce by an exhilarating jaunt on the ferry to Staten Island—which by the way, offers a tremendous view of The Statue of Liberty.

I scanned dozens of passages informing that vampires, due to their soulless nature, could no longer cast their reflections in mirrors. False. That vampires could be repelled by the sign of the Christian Cross ... disproved as my eye lingered upon the silver crucifix which dangled languidly above the breasts of the young librarian who often came on shift during my late evening research. She bore something of a resemblance to my Deirdre, and I'd catch myself from time to time entranced by her supple movements. She was so very, very much alive.

As for causes of vampiredom there were here amassed a truly absurd plenitude. You might become a vampire, for instance, if a cat had leapt over your corpse before burial. If a curse was placed upon you, or some ancestor, by any number of religious personages you might also be subdued; especially if you had been excommunicated from The Church—where it was recorded Christian doctrine that after you died in such a state, "Ye shoulde finde no rest."

A seventh child born to mutual parents had the potential to return from death a vampire, and the seventh child to a seventh child was doubly endangered. Murderers, those murdered, and especially suicides could reawaken as vampires. People who sported both red hair and blue eyes ran an elevated risk as well.

If either a dead or doomed man's glance chance fell upon you, say from a man being prepared for the gallows, then you'd be in jeopardy. Reportedly, that's why they cover the dead, or those soon to be dead, with shrouds or hoods or in some instances, with blindfolds.

Vampirism supposedly could be inherited, that suggested some form of spiritual genetics. And one of my favorites, that anyone who was previously afflicted during their lifetime by the irksome transformative affliction of lycanthropy (that of being a weirwolf) would surely return after death as a vampire. Furthermore, on the subject of transmography there were numerous accounts of the vampires' ability to permutate into a thick fog, a wolf, a bat, or even in one quite poetic account I'd read, into a butterfly.

If you were born on a Saturday, the day of the Old Testament's Sabbath, then it was presupposed you could *never* be killed by a vampire, nor had you any danger of ever becoming one, which subsequently made you quite a meritorious candidate to become a vampire hunter.

Of course, were a person to be untimely dispatched by a vampire, he or she would in due course return in a like state.

Several variations exist concerning this indoctrination, which range from the necessity of the presence of a full moon at the time of slaughter to the victim's willing re-ingestion of their own blood to promulgate a vampiric rebirth.

In addition, there were certain inherent powers that would be supposedly vested within the vampire, none of which I've yet to demonstrate; such as invisibility, telekinesis, astral projection, hypnosis, and numerous methods of self-induced flight. I scoffed in regard to these books with their tremendous depth of lack of knowledge on the subject ... especially in regard to the fictional works that dared to romanticize the afterlife of the *un*dead. Charlatans all!

Page after page and account after gore-filled account I rummaged for the slightest hint of truth, for surely there were indeed vampires out there, as my existence attested to me with disparaging clarity, and surely there must have been legitimate sightings recorded. Surely. Perhaps there some seldom handled, title-whispered text rendered by the trembling hand of some rapturous clergyman and now sequestered away in some dark labyrinth caverns beneath the holy chambers of Rome. Surely something was written down someplace, for God's sake!

FOR ALL THE DELUSIONS, fabrications, and all too transparent misinterpretations that I encountered within recorded literature upon the subject of vampires, one undeniable truth had eventually wormed its way up through the soil of my awareness:

Whether they are referred to as *Umpir* from Russia, or *Vrikolax* from Greece, call them the *Nachzehrer* of Northern Germany or the *Strigoi* of Rumania, the *Kiang-si* of China or the *Rakshasha* of India, all are blood drinkers. What made itself so clear to me then was that these sightings, these myths, these phantasms had each developed separately throughout the world, within cultures that varied by virtually unbreachable gulfs during their arcane inceptions, and yet each pointed a clear collective finger at me.

One particularly troubling evening I had risen early, around 6:35 PM, and made my way perilously up towards Central Park. It was just prior to sunset, and in my own somewhat twisted version of hide and go seek I allowed the shade of the buildings to fend off the final lethal rays. This was the first time I'd set foot in the park since we'd died, and upon entering I experienced a tremor of nostalgic homecoming. Nature's final vestige within Manhattan, a place where people could now and again shake loose the burdens of metropolis. For me, it was like a slice of that small town upstate from which I was so untimely ripped. Chelsea and I used to run around in the woods with our friends until long after dark during the summer ...

I found myself a nice spot beneath an oak to sit and read some case studies I was excited about. For you see, my existence had now been reduced to the simple pleasurable acts of reading, sleeping, and observing the wellspring of life around me. There, beneath my tree, branches searching out above my head like some protective gesture, I sat reading a translation of a Serbian textbook of the occult by twilight that I'd borrowed from a rather poorly secured display case at the Serbo-Croatian Historical Society.

It was barely a book by this time due to the dilapidated condition of the spine, now reduced to irregular sections of loose yellowed pages; so brittle that they cracked and threatened to crumble beneath the weight of my scrolling fingers.

Here I found a reference to a subject that finally piqued my interest, a reference made that had never been mentioned in the countless texts I'd read before. It was a court-transcribed testimonial of an acquitted murderer who had been accused of decapitating a man before witnesses in front of the town hall. The acquittal was reportedly due to an overwhelming public consensus that the deceased had been a vampire. An evil man who had been laid to rest seven days earlier, again before witnesses. Therefore, the defense claimed that the man, already dead, could not have been murdered. Furthermore, the man accused of decapitating him was in actuality carrying out the prescribed religious duties of his sacred blood ancestral post.

The Court Clergyman then referred to the accused murderer by the peculiar designation of a "Damphyre."

I looked up from the text with the bizarre predilection that within that very word *Damphyre*, some revelation of my vampiric mutation must arise. There was something familiarly haunting about that word. Damphyre ...

In that moment which held such great promise I looked up and became aware of two young children, a boy and a girl no older than six or seven, who were playing ball together alarmingly near the secluded grove in which I sat. I guess upon reflection I should have thought it odd that I did not detect their parents and it was growing quite dark. Nor did I immediately spring to remove myself from a site that could at any moment be overtaken with people. I guess at the time I was not to be shaken away from the text that I held, and the tableau of that young boy and girl laughing and kicking the ball back and forth was like some half-dreamt mirage conjured up from my memory. They seemed to be having a wonderful time of it; though, from the intermittent squeals that she made.

I read on in nervous, frenzied anticipation, with decreasing amounts of awareness as my eyes scanned the pages for any recurrence of the term *Damphyre*: "Wooden stake ... buried face down at a crossroads, carcass burdened asunder by stones of tremendous weight ... nails driven into both skull and heart ... coins in the mouth ... hands and feet bound with thorned vines ... yet still the corpse did rise again, and hence they dispatched for a Damphyre ..."

Through the corner of my eye I saw the children's ball now lay abandoned in the grass ... as I read onward:

"The Damphyre arrived posthaste and was vested of all manner of supernatural charms to overpower the murderous vampyre. He was a man of most unnatural health, pallid skin, rutted cheeks, and thin of bone, almost as though he were a revenant himself. He then proclaimed before the villagers that indeed he was descended from the seed of a vampyre sewn within the belly of a human mother. And being thus born had been tasked with the slaying of vampyres, the only trade in which the Lord might will his hands to prosper. He could track the vampyre always without fail, for the bond of his kinship with them was such that he could recognize them even had they made themselves invisible. The Damphyre could never take any direct payment for his services, as each cleansing act he performed was then offered up to God as penance ..."

At this point a shrill scream tore me away from my reading.

I beheld the menacing strike pose taken by the young boy who now cobralike bore back his fangs and prepared to attack the young girl. She screamed again, this time more faintly, and a wave of enjoyment appeared to wash over the boy's features for that split second before he lunged and struck.

I was up off the ground in a mad dash for them as the force of his impact sent them both tumbling to the ground with his mouth grappled vicelike on her throat.

How dreadful that I should have failed to notice him for what he was, that smell, the lack of heartbeats!

Reaching them, I immediately ripped him away from her and sent his body sprawling off a good length where he knocked solidly against a tree and let loose a frightened, defensive growl. The little girl was opened slightly at the neck, though he hadn't the time to fatally wound her. She'd more than likely live.

A woman stepped into our clearing and let out an unnervingly loud scream, and the young vampire turned on his heel and sped off through the woods. I hesitated a moment, before I turned and tore off after him.

He was remarkably fleet, supranaturally so, and had I not held twice his gait, by length of leg alone, he would have easily lost me dodging in and out of groves of trees. We entered the lesser traveled woods beyond the paths and I saw him snapping back a look to see if I was still chasing him. His face was a mask of terror and I remember thinking, *Who has done this? Who dared to make a little boy into a wild beast?*

"Don't hurt me!" he screamed as he ran. "Don't hurt! Don't hurt! Don't hurt me please don't hurt!"

I caught up just behind him, reached out and grabbed him by the shoulder, spinning and slamming him into a small outcrop of rock. With a tremendous desperation the child then turned and with the ferocity of a cat that's been cornered, began violently lashing out at me with hands that hit like steel knives.

I saw my stomach open up from his slashes, and I slashed back at him reflexively, opening several large gashes on him in return. We ripped, we tore, we cleaved and we shredded each other. Then finally, I ducked in low, feinted him and moved to scoop his small body from behind the knees. I lifted him high overhead, twisted my body and sent him crashing hard face first into the ground, and then came crashing down atop him. I think I broke his back.

I pushed off and disentangled myself from the boy who now lay twisted and heaving, great spasms of pain contorting the once fine features of his face. He managed to drag himself a few feet away and then rolled to one side and stared back at me with great luminous bloodshot eyes that seemed to plead, *"Help, help me. I'm all broken can't you see?"*

I looked down at over a dozen cross rips that he'd opened up along the length of my body. Already I was chanting under my breath and they had begun to mend themselves. But the boy? I didn't know if he would be able to heal himself or not, there was so much about *them* I just didn't know. The wounds that I'd opened upon his small form—which now almost seemed delicate as he lay still—

bled out with swift profusion all the stolen blood that he'd amassed over who knows how long.

He let out a soft moan and continued to stare up at me. I saw him run his tongue feebly across his thin eyeteeth. This was no book, I remember thinking. This was really one of *them*.

I got my pain under control after a time and knew that soon I would be able to stand. It would only be a short time before we would be found—and what if we should be found?

Then miraculously, the kid managed to raise himself up to his knees through great spasms of pain, suggesting that he also had some powers of rejuvenation. Eye on me with each and every movement, down on all fours, he began digging at the earth with his hands. As I watched him, I became suddenly aware of his intentions; of course, he wanted to bury himself in the earth!

I wondered whether I should move to prevent him from doing so, or if I should assist him? A thousand arguments attacked me *en masse*, and I didn't know what to do. *Try to kill him? Was he not life? But didn't he live by stealing the lives of others? Would he not do so again were I to leave him here? Was I supposed to drag him back up to the apartment and tell this six-year-old killer to sit back and meditate?*

He was digging a grave for himself as fast as he could. I watched with intense fascination how life, no matter how corrupt the form, will seek out any means at hand for preservation.

Then abruptly something changed in the boy. A wave of calm swept over him and he stopped digging and appeared to be listening intently to something that I couldn't hear. Then he turned to me and cocked his head to one side as if he was trying to fathom me. I wondered what he might be seeing, perhaps the lack of blood, or maybe the range of revulsion and compassion that I was feeling for him?

For an instant, I swear a look of inner peace flowed through those infant eyes.

And then without warning he burst into blistering flames.

I got up and I got the hell out of there.

9

The Ministry.

An organization whose very existence is such a dreadful rumor nervously whispered amidst the global law enforcement community—a specter in their gears. And if that whisper just happens to materialize in your neck of the woods, whether you're CIA, KGB, MI5, Interpol, or perhaps some lesser-known authority, then it's more than likely in your best interest to back yourself out of that whisper's way.

The Ministry, an entirely self-contained international bureau of investigation which has never been either officially sanctioned nor publicly recognized by a single nation or government yet granted instant and unchallenged sovereignty over any paranormal-related investigation at any place or at any time.

The Ministry, with its satellite monasteries rifling through the masses in search of those precious few men and women who can withstand being pushed far enough along the path of enlightenment to slow the exponential growth of our vampiric transformation.

The Ministry—bane of the vampire.

A twelve-foot-long bronze plaque hangs prominently upon the wall in the main communications concourse of the New York office that reads, "Sacrifice even your own liberation until all sentient beings are free from suffering." A phrase translated from Sanskrit, written some two thousand years ago in India by a Zen master named Nagarjuna. It's been strategically placed so that upon entering the concourse from any of its six entrances you can't help but see it.

"Sacrifice even your own liberation until all sentient beings are free from suffering." A powerful suggestion to receive before one takes up the responsibilities of one's evening shift.

Observe the two agents who diligently man their command post amidst a myriad of flashing lights, denoting incoming communications. Proud, dedicated, compassionate souls who are seeking their path to enlightenment through their service. One of them, a lovely young woman named Clarice, is a personal friend of mine. Watch as her lips move with grace and confidence as she calls through the headset that's half hidden beneath her hair, "New York office is clear. How copy, Bangkok?"

"Roger, New York. What is your current residence?"

"Current residence is nine, Bangkok. Repeat, nine."

"Copy, New York. Sun is up. Signing off. Have a clear night."

"Copy. Thanks."

"Bangkok, over and out."

Nine, she'd said. Somewhere within the confines of these grounds there are nine vampire Slayers who have ascended beyond the rank of third level Initiate. Eight of them having willingly given up their entire lives for this cause of protecting humanity from infection. *Why are they here? What gives one the prescribed will to enter this spectral convent? Could I have ever made such a conscious choice myself?* This question eternally ravages me.

There, behind that desk, sits Clarice, a woman I've known for some time, hunted alongside. As a teen she was gang-raped and beaten to the point of total amnesia, and was later shuttled from foster home to foster home on a violent train of drug abuse and casual abandonment. There she sits immersed with compassion for her fellow man as she sips her cup of coffee and smiles at her shift-mate. *From where did she come by the strength?*

The idea that these people are drawn to protect their helpless and unsuspecting brethren at risk to their very lives (perchance to their souls), night after night, seems almost implausible in relation to the apathy of the majority of humankind. To these soldiers I bear a reverence unsurpassed.

"Sacrifice even your own liberation until all sentient beings are free from suffering," the plaque reads. Let me tell you about the first time, nearly four years ago, that I first sat bound and gagged beneath it.

It had been several rather uneventful months since the Central Park incident, uneventful in that I had made no further contacts, although not for lack of trying on my part. I needed to find one of *them* that was capable of holding some dialogue with me. I had to know why this was allowed to happen to people and what it was exactly that was happening to me.

Like a man who'd been forcibly stranded on a deserted isle, I longed for the company of my peers even as I dreaded the very thought of their existence. It was then that I began to fear my own objectives. For at the base of my intentions wasn't I desirous of mingling in the company of depraved butchers?

I sat vigil through each night to find *them* in the downtown alleyways where drunks would stumble about to relieve themselves, such easy prey, and on the near deserted subway platforms, during the twilight hours, still so rich with their lingering scents of the previous day. No vampires came. Though, in my paranoia they were always lurking there behind that pillar at the corner of my eye. Nobody wanted to play with me.

Each day I awoke in the apartment, checked that the place had not during the day been violated, and then spent at least one hour in the nourishment of meditation. I made a traveling kit to bring along on my watch that comprised of two or three books to read, a notebook and pen, some cosmetics and a small transistor radio I'd stolen. Empty months slipped past ... and then came the night the routine broke.

I was up on a fire escape of a building on the West side at Fifty-Third Street at approximately three in the morning. That height afforded a clear view of an all-night liquor store and several adjoining alleyways. I observed a man, elderly and perhaps homeless, enter and subsequently leave the store now carrying a brown paper bag which I can only assume held a bottle of liquor. As the man left the store he was approached and greeted by another man, with whom he seemed unfamiliar and from whom I personally perceived an unsettling presence of malicious intent. The two came to some form of mutual agreement and then turned a corner together and entered the series of alleyways. My view of them became obscured and I was forced to descend from the fire escape, cursing myself for not reacting sooner.

I reached ground level and rapidly made my way towards the direction in which they had turned. Then I felt *him*, there, just around the corner, just a few feet from the place where I now stood. I hesitated, couldn't bring myself to turn the corner. I put my back to the wall out of indecision and tried to psyche myself up, build my courage.

Then this *feeling* came slithering, like mangled fingers creeping spiderlike around that wall towards me like some horrible black void of space that seemed to swallow light as it moved. I didn't know whether to scream for help or run for my life. But I kept telling myself that it was here that I had striven to be, in the presence of one of *them*.

And then, a sound that I swear shall stay with me through each waking hour of the rest of my sentient days. A furious and throaty *suck-suck*ing sound accompanied by agonized moans.

I forced myself through the overwhelming dread and turned the corner. There on the ground, I beheld the horrific act itself in all of its naked clarity.

The man was sprawled in sewage, face up and feebly scraping at the head of the thing which was straddling his stomach and locked like a vise to his throat.

The vampire's entire body heaved furiously up and down as it sucked and siphoned the fluid from the man's body. Rivulets of blood escaped from the gaping wound and its tongue flicked about in rabid spasms to retrieve them. I wanted to retch, or to tear myself away from the spectacle, but I couldn't.

I believe *it* was too enthralled in its feeding to notice me as I just stood there agape before this blasphemous coupling. There was little to no possibility of helping the man to survive at this point, even if I hadn't been frozen still with terror. The thing just kept on sucking and glutting itself until I was sure that no more blood could come from the wound and yet the steady flow continued on and on and on until the fury of the suction finally reached a crescendo and the vampire shuddered and released its hold upon the man's neck.

I was startled back a few steps and got myself into the deep shadows. The thing still didn't see me. And now I thought, surely it must be done, but it wasn't over yet. Now, the monster bent low and began to lick the spilt blood from the face and chest of the man, finally lapping its tongue in the bloody puddle on the mucky ground, so insatiable was its appetite!

Horrorstruck, I backed myself further away from the scene. Around the corner, out of view. I shut my eyes and started mouthing the mantra.

Then there were clattering footfalls as the vampire sped away from its kill, to which I had no other obvious response at the time but to follow.

———————

AT HALF PAST three I found myself following the vampire into a Westside dive of a bar called Carmilla's Kitchen. It was packed tight with people, bright lights, and awash in the scents of perfumes, cigarettes, and alcohol. I lost sight of him momentarily as a girl asked me if I'd wanted my coat checked. I motioned her away, and moved myself through the hard press of bodies toward the back of the bar. There at the far end, I noted a staircase leading down. I was hoping that was where he'd gone, because I couldn't spot him anywhere on this floor.

A stocky young man seated on a stool before the staircase, whose eyes were repeatedly scanning the crowd, presented an immediate problem. Those stairs obviously led to a more exclusive club.

I moved up to the bar and placed my back to him. *Can't lose him now!* I remember thinking to myself. *Too damn close!*

The bartender, a heavyset man wearing an eye patch, approached me and asked what I might like to drink, informing me that whiskey shots were now, "two for one." I told him I wasn't ready to order just yet, and he moved on down the line. Then a hand brushed my shoulder from off to my left and a deep, pleasant voice asked, "Hey friend, buy you a drink?"

The contact momentarily shocked me, though I tried as best I could to mask my hypersensitivity as I turned to face the voice. He was a tall, thin man in his thirties, I'd guessed, solidly built, with short brown hair and what I first presumed to be a drunken grin. He wore a black leather jacket over blue jeans, and well-worn cowboy boots. His unapologetic stare gave me the impression he wanted something more from me than casual conversation. Whatever it was, I certainly had no time for it.

"Thanks, no," I replied, with a careful concealment of teeth.

"I hear there's another bar downstairs that really kicks," he said then. "Is that where you're headed? Cause if you are, I'm really interested in going down there myself." His grin became a smirk, and he clumsily slipped off his stool.

I grew alarmed by the fact that there was no trace of alcohol on this man's breath. He was feigning drunkenness for my benefit. "No, sorry," I told him. "I'm waiting for someone."

"Don't wait too long, friend," he said as he turned to go.

He had been most definitively human. *Why would he have wanted to go where the vampire had gone? I wondered. Or had he just been following my gaze? And where was the vampire? There could be several exits downstairs and I might have lost him already! I'm going to have to try and get past the man at the stairs now!*

I put on a dopey smile and moved directly towards the stocky young man on the stool who wore bright red suspenders and now sipped with cool calculation from a frosted glass of beer. Drinking meant human, which I decided was somehow in my favor. He regarded me through wolfish eyes as I calmly approached, as one of those people who were apparently trained in the art of body language. I noted with some trepidation that he held within his left hand a shiny metal box with a black button at its center upon which his thumb was tensely poised. A thin wire snaked from the back of said box and slithered its way down behind him.

As I neared him, I gave him full eye contact and noted that his gaze was returned not to my eyes but just a couple inches below them. *He's watching my mouth,* I realized. *He's watching my mouth to see whether I'm human or not!*

I flashed him my eyeteeth, and his thumb came off the button. The realization that I was a vampire actually relaxed his features, contrary to what one might expect. He gave me a dip-of-the-chin nod with a humble demeanor; indicating that I should go right on ahead. I nodded back and passed by him, relieved. And then I was faced with the stairway leading down into pitch black. My eyes adjusted, and I began my slow descent.

At the bottom of the stairs I came to a heavy oak door that had the word *Hell* written across it in red lipstick. When I say that the door was heavy, I mean that its opening required a great deal of force, so much so in fact, that I'm doubtful the average man could have pushed it open. *Hell* was right ...

First came the rancid smell, nearly overpowering, washing past me. There was perhaps a dozen of *them*, all vampires by first glance, milling about languidly to the droll of some pulse-maddening music. A few of them glanced my way, then went back to what they'd been doing.

They thought I was just another one of them.

Tending the bar there were several humans, all females, none older than I had been at my turning. They moved with unnatural slowness and each stood in various stages of leaking out their own blood, through the various wounds that they appeared to be self-inflicting, into a plethora of crystal decanters that lined the bar.

Mother of God! I thought. *Where am I?*

I just stood there aghast by the way some petite redhead nonchalantly opened her wrist with a straight razor, letting her juices run free for a moment into the rim of a glass, then stopped the flow with a piece of gauze. Then she offered the glass to a gray-haired monstrosity who leered at her and then blew her a kiss before quaffing her blood down in a single swill before her glazed stare.

"I don't know you," suddenly broke my attention. This from one of *them* who had stepped up beside me. *This is showtime,* I thought at that moment. *Time to control your fear or get yourself killed, or worse! A moment of great risk and of great opportunity!* "I wonder if we might have a word at my table?"

He was similar to me in both height and build, but that's where the resemblance ended. His arms appeared elongated and disproportionate to his form as he led me over towards a small, secluded booth. I watched him move, and noted his gait was somewhat unsteady, as though with each step he was dragging along some tremendous weight.

"Please, sit," came his voice again, a deep vibrato which reverberated briefly as he spoke, like the echo of a poorly connected long-distance telephone call. "I make it my personal business to meet each dark brother who enters the city. No one here has seen you before. Inquiries are flying all over the place. But, excuse my manners, do you thirst?"

"No," I replied, attempting to match his manner, his vibrato. "I find I am sufficiently filled."

"Excellent," he said, grinning and then reclining back in his chair. "You do indeed appear *sufficiently filled*, Dark Brother."

He then began to chuckle to himself in a manner that in a human I'd have taken for an advanced stage of drunkenness. And then it dawned on me that *yes, this just might be the case,* this creature sitting across from me here was indeed drunk. Drunk on blood. My hopes of pumping him for information rose tremendously as did my chances, I supposed, of leaving this dungeon unscathed.

I took a closer look at its face now, the fears that I had of meeting the gaze of a true beast quickly vanishing. The face still held traces of what had been human once, but all those marks that could reflect human vitality and human character were gone; replaced by a corpselike frigidity. I attribute the fact that there was but the barest glint of health beneath his flesh to the tremendous amount of blood he had obviously just imbibed.

His canines were apparent as he spoke, and his bloodstained teeth seemed somewhat larger, perhaps sharper than mine, perhaps due to their blasphemous misuse. However, the feature that stood out upon him, so awful and clear an image to date within my mind's eye, was a bizarre series of twisted scars that ringed the circumference of his lips as if they had somehow been cleaved and repeatedly punctured.

He noticed me staring and then almost absent-mindedly ran his own fingers along the lacerations. "Never seen these marks before?" he remarked in a faraway tone. I shrugged. "Not all that surprising. Not too many of us still around, lot of burnouts. Rumania, seventeenth century, they called us Strigoi, used to sew up the mouths of the corpses with heavy fishing line, cat gut, so we wouldn't be able to open them. Had to tear the stitches out with my fingers. Wounds never heal. Eyes sewn up too, look."

The vampire shut his eyes for a moment and I observed similar puncture wounds across each set of eyelids.

"So we wouldn't be able to see," he continued, "when we were finally strong enough to dig ourselves out of the earth. Damned peasants. I find that I can never drink enough of peasants."

Then he made a flashing motion towards the bar which I did not understand. A young ash-blonde saw this signal and hesitated, a wing of fear brushing her features momentarily before she moved off from the bar and started towards us.

A fear rose within me. A fear that was born for this girl. It was one thing to sit there, feigning calm, putting myself at risk. But what horrors could I endure before my very eyes without response in this sanctum of death? I was trapped. Whatever his intentions were, I was just as trapped here as she was.

She moved fearfully up to the table and stopped. I looked into a pair of stricken light-blue eyes that reflected a vast and desolate landscape of fear. She knew. Somehow, she sensed that she had only moments to live. She thought about running, but knew there was no place to run. In that brief moment of contact, I sent my heart out to her in silent soul speech.

I told her I was sorry that her life would end this way, that I was powerless to help, that I believed there was life after death.

Her eyes were awash in tears that revealed her to me in truly overwhelming waves of returned acceptance. She belonged at her parents' house safe in bed, damn it! Not here, sleeping all day and letting them spill out her blood at night in a drained stupor. She should be out on a date with some boyfriend and spilling out love and affection and looking forward to life and a home and someday a family of her own. I truly felt that we were somehow communicating. As if the nearness of her death had provided some sort of bridge. *Goodbye, poor sweet child. I'm so sorry. Goodbye.*

The vampire then reached up his hand, grasped her hair and said, "Come little peasant, I thirst!"

One quick, sharp pull and he brought her fragile head crashing down like a thunderclap onto our tabletop. Her face demolished into a pulp from the heavy impact amidst the shattered glass.

I just sat there motionless, as he gingerly lapped at the spray of her blood from the back of his hand. From somewhere nearby, I heard shrill vampiric laughter and the sound of glasses clinking. The music throbbed on. There was nothing I could have done.

A few moments later, the first assault team exploded in.

———————

DOORS CRASHED INWARD from somewhere back behind the bar and vampires sprang to their feet in alarm all about me. Smoke began filling the room. The drunken revenant seated across from me suddenly sobered, eyes wide toward the forward entrance— which was rammed open moments later.

The man who forced the door was that grinning, soft-spoken man in the leather jacket who'd talked with me earlier, minus the grin. He forced the button-wielding watchdog from the head of the stairs through the entrance as a shield in front of himself. There was blood on his shirt-front. *But you're only human!* I wanted to scream. *What do you think you're going to do to* Them?

Behind the man stood three other men who came suddenly pouring into the room, all humans.

From somewhere a vampiric screech, "MINISTRY!"

The entire room burst into movement. I stood transfixed by the brown-haired man. He flung his prisoner ahead of him into a slashing whirlwind of a vampire that was rushing headlong toward him.

The vampire dodged past the watchdog and slashed out with breakneck speed, connecting and drawing blood out of the brown-haired man's left shoulder. I expected the man to go down, to drop off—how could a mere man stand face-to-face with one of these monsters?

But that man did not go down, nor did he seem to recognize the fact that he'd been cut. His right hand, now a blur, produced what looked to me like a wooden stake, whipped it around and sunk it deep in the chest of the vampire! The vampire wailed like a wounded animal, grasping and flailing to pull the thing out of its chest.

Then the man clutched the stake and tore it loose again, like a plug that was suddenly popped from a drain, and the vampire cried out once more. Then it fell to its knees. I was terrified, and I was awestruck.

Now, I heard similar wails from all about the room as other vampires fell by the hands of these men called *Ministry*. Then the vampire who'd been standing by my side shouted, "Run or be slain, brother!" and then fled the room. I couldn't help but watch the carnage. It was like watching a film. I was captivated. I think I may have even sat back down for a moment as I watched.

Then, one of these Ministry men cornered the one that I had followed down here in the first place, the one from the liquor store. It slashed and thrashed in wild continuous motions, daring the man to come closer, to enter its reach. The man stayed cool, kept his staking arm loose and fluid, and I could tell he was just waiting for a clear shot.

A scream called my attention behind the bar where a female vampire fended off one of the men by holding a barmaid before her, as a shield, threatening to rend the girl in two with her bloody nails digging into the girl's bare stomach.

Then from the corner of my eye, I saw the brown-haired Ministry man exit the fray, bounding up the stairs the way he'd come. Without hesitation, I was out of my seat and after him.

When I reached the ground level, I was momentarily

thrown by the emptiness of the place ... just half an hour ago there had been throngs of drunken, dancing people. They'd left the music playing. *And just how close was it to sunrise, now?* I wondered, as I raced outside. The brown-haired man was nowhere in sight.

Then a strong, imploring voice assailed me. "Gentle one," the voice said. "Please, turn to face me."

I turned to behold one of the most beautiful human beings I have ever seen. He was of an indeterminate old age, and radiated a soft blue ethereal glow. For a moment, I was filled with a kind of religious fervor. I thought maybe he was an angel. But then I saw the lifeforce pumping through his face and knew he was a man. He wore a gray robe, clasped at the neck, and radiated wisdom through his simple countenance. He smiled at me with a warmth akin to an old friend just returned from a very long journey.

I looked down at the ground and saw there were seven neat piles of ash scattered upon the pavement where he stood. It took me a moment to recognize what these piles must have been, perhaps only several moments earlier. *Reduced to ashes! My God!* I thought.

"*I deliver upon you a message, Gentle One,*" the angelic man said. "*You have our blessings, and harm yourself not. These new things you have learnt shall bode well for all things. The changes you now perceive as accidents were indeed no accidents. Each turn of your life has been inspired by this course which you now shall follow. Seek to teach the lessons you've unlearned.*"

"Who are you people?" I exclaimed, dumbly.

His reply was to nimbly turn and round the corner, disappearing from sight. Again, I took to pursuit and came around the side of the building in a run. Rounding the next corner, I nearly slammed into the brown-haired man.

He had several of his team with him now, and everyone froze in their tracks. Six wooden stakes were drawn at various points all around me. Yet the stake of the brown-haired man remained sheathed at his side. He regarded me once more, as he had in the bar through those distinct blue-gray eyes of his.

"Hold it," he called, raising his hand to the others. "I want this one taken, not slain." Then to me he asked, "Will you consent to be taken, or do we stake you here and now?"

I smiled at the brashness of his confidence. "That's the clearest two choices I've been offered in God-only-knows-how-long," I told him. "Mind telling me your name? I didn't catch it at the bar."

The others were nervous, astounded, confused. I guessed then that conversations between humans and vampires were uncommon events. The stakes, however, perhaps now relaxed, were not going down. I got a chill as I wondered what one of them might feel like if it entered my body. The idea both frightened and delighted me.

"Garett," he said. "The name's Garett."

"Well then, Garett," I replied. "I guess I'll surrender."

He grinned at me, and then, "Bind him!" he barked.

Three of them held me as I was frisked, then shackled with heavy chain that came out of the trunk of one of their cars. And then one of them jammed a thick and foul-tasting rubber device into my mouth that made any jaw movements next to impossible.

I saw two surviving barmaids, their clothing damp with blood, carried roughly from the rear entrance of the bar and dropped in the back of a van, which then quickly sped off.

There was another van, for those who were dead, which remained on the scene. I was disturbed to notice that one of the Ministry men was in the process of binding the legs and wrists of the dead girls with heavy steel wire.

Then two men lifted me up and dropped me in the trunk of a car. The last thing I remember seeing before someone slammed the lid down was Garett, speaking into a very compact walkie-talkie.

He said, "The Den is raked. Copy control, I repeat. The Den is raked."

———————

AN HOUR later I found myself still bound, with the terrible device still inserted in my mouth. I was seated within a large, windowless, cathedral-ceilinged hall at a small wooden desk. High overhead there was an enormous bronze plaque set deep within the smooth gray marble. The plaque read, "Sacrifice even your own liberation until all sentient beings are free from suffering." Good words, I remember thinking, although the gag was choking me.

One of the Ministry men, a muscular chap in black coveralls, knelt by my side mouthing obscenities at me, whilst Garett, his obvious superior, stood off at some distance and eyed me with curious speculation. I wanted the gag out badly. I wanted to explain myself to him. Explain that I was no killer, and that I abhorred the vampires with the same disgust that he did. I couldn't speak, but held on to the belief that once they let me (if they let me) there was hope of our reaching some sort of understanding. I supposed the fact that I had not been staked was a point already in my favor. But how could I make him believe me?

"Silver-tongued butcher, that's what you are, you scum!" said the man in black coveralls. "How many lives have you drunk down that fetid little throat of yours, huh? Oh man, I wanna stake you so bad I can barely contain myself!" At this he produced his stake. Then he gripped and spun it around like some gunslinger dexterously twirling his gun, and held it before my face.

"That's as close as you get, Craig," Garett intervened.

And the Ministry man sheathed his stake.

"What are we saving him for?" he asked after a time. "Because he was too chicken shit to go out fighting? Hell, he probably could've taken one or two of us out with him. They're just gonna send him upstate to a farm and let some other disciple go at him anyway."

"Not your place to judge," he told Craig. "And if that's the case then so be it. Another disciple faces the Blackened Gate."

"But this depraved bastard's not even a worthy test!"

Garett met my gaze again with that penetrating stare of his.

"Maybe," he said. "Maybe more of a test than you think."

Craig laughed. "What's eating you?"

"I don't know. But it sure is hungry."

"So, what are we waiting on?"

"I sent for a Master."

"*Jesus*, why'd you do that?"

"Gut feeling. There's something wrong here."

"Who's coming down?"

"Kamala."

"Kamala, huh?"

"Yes, sir."

"Well then, my bloodsucking friend," Craig said, now turning back towards me. "You're about to come face-to-face with a Master. You might just get to know how Joan of Arc felt before she went out. You might wish that you'd gone down by one of us."

Then there were footsteps behind me. Both men looked past me at whomever was approaching and immediately bowed down their heads in supplication.

I heard a crisp, vibrant voice project, "Gentlemen, what issue have we here that requires my attention?"

I opened my eyes as a squat, East Indian man with a kind, cherub face, dressed like a monk, came around me to clasp hands with Craig, then embrace Garett. I saw lights about him that were similar to those of the man in gray robes who had halted me in front of the bar. My heart unexpectedly rose.

"Something about this one I don't comprehend, Master," Garett explained. "Forgive me for rousing you due to my ignorance."

"Nonsense," the glowing man said. "I am ever your servant, my humblest of students. Now, let me attend to this creature which troubles you so."

At this, the man they called Master turned back to me, and met my eyes.

See me, I demanded through my returned gaze, trying to broadcast my thoughts, *truly see me and know that I'm not a killer!*

I tried, hard as I could, to show him the pain I had known, the hell I'd faced just to get here. I did this in the hope some psychic ability lived in this man they called *Master*, who seemingly now held my fate in his hands. I broadcast my will through my eyes.

His face flustered and fluidly altered as he continued probing me and then ... we connected. *Communion!* It was a warm, beautiful, most welcomed spiritual contact.

Through a sob, he called, *"By the Twelve, Garett, release him!"*

Garett seemed about to protest but thought better of it, then glancing towards the countenance of his teacher, obeyed and removed the dreadful device from my mouth. Then he unbound my arms and my legs. Craig backed away from the scene in distress, wildly confused, cupping a hand to his mouth.

"Thank you," was all I could manage to say, as I rubbed at my wrists and stretched my jaw.

The Master Kamala then bowed down his head and whispered, "Forgive me. Forgive them. Forgive us, we ... dear friend, I stand here before you in reverence and awe."

Garett moved now in between us and grasped hard onto Kamala's shoulder. "Master, forgive me," he began in earnest. "Does he have you under some sort of spell?"

To which Kamala replied by gently turning him back toward me, "See ... look to him, see not his form but delve inwards. Look through the eye of the mind. What do you see?"

A wave of confusion washed over Garett; his features contorted. He took an unconfident step backwards. "There's no blood ..." he mumbled. "He moves from the ocean of *Chi!*"

His legs went weak and Garett fell down to one knee. Then a shiver seemed to strike him once, and then again.

"Please forgive my young student, my friend. He is now passing through, as I have just passed through, and as many shall soon pass through upon recognition of you, a state of awakening that we refer to as *satori*. In you we find paradox that should not be possible, yet here you sit. The implications that manifest even now within me are staggering ... staggering."

"I'm happy to see you folks, too."

"Forgive me," Kamala said, shaking his head in embarrassment. "Do you have any special needs to which we might attend before I leave to communicate word of your ... *arrival?*"

"Well, Sir, I do have one request," I said. "The sun's about to come up. Any minute now. Could you see fit to provide me with a secure, enclosed room where I might sleep?"

"Certainly," he said, with a smile of astonishment. "I shall see to it personally. And I shall see you lie undisturbed until nightfall."

"Thank you, Kamala. It feels like I've found my way to a very good place."

"Indeed," he replied, and then held out his hands to clasp mine in the first gentle contact I'd made since my death. It felt good. "Welcome dear friend, to the Ministry."

10

I Sense within this vampiric form before me the wisdom light of the *Way* and an Adept of the Art of Slaying Vampires," were the words of the Master of Masters, an ancient Chinese man named Choi Leung, who had presided over my, for lack of a better word, interrogation.

We had traveled by limousine several hours upstate, Kamala and I, because Choi Leung was of failing health, and would not have been able to make the journey himself. As we drove up, I told him some of the details about my life. He sat, listened, and nodded from time to time. "I'm amazed," I told him at the conclusion, "by what I've seen you people do."

"Not so amazed," he countered, "as the Masters shall soon be by you. Really, I should have allowed you to read today's message transcription. I had six men guard your door all day for fear you might be besieged. Patience, I'm afraid, is not one of the Ministry's virtues."

The car brought us up to the main entrance of the Calverton Monastery and honked its horn twice. We got out and walked toward the main entrance, past an immaculate lawn and row after row of well-tended flower beds. "This may be tedious, my friend," Kamala said as we walked, "So, please bear in mind that you are like a gateway for us. A gateway that promises ascension to a higher level of comprehension within our sacred order."

"If you say so," I shrugged. "May I ask them questions as well?"

"Surely, they shall welcome your questions as I do. For your questions may reveal much, if not more, than your answers to their questions."

"And the blind one, the old man, he shall decide in the end?"

"Fear not Choi Leung's fire, my friend. You have nothing in you whatsoever to burn."

We entered a large unattended hall and proceeded past several empty chambers. "I imagined that there would be scores of monks running about," I whispered.

"All off grounds," he replied. "No disciples are permitted to make any contact with you until Choi Leung is satisfied. Here we are. Are you ready?"

I nodded, and he knocked gently upon a heavy wooden door.

"Come," came an instant response.

We entered a large meditation room, sparsely furnished and illuminated solely by candlelight. There they sat on the floor, eleven Masters of the Art of Slaying Vampires, the most I would ever see congregated in one place, for one purpose. In this case, apparent by their collective gaze, that purpose being me. As both Kamala and the mystery Master I'd met before him seemed to radiate some kind of energy, or aura, so did these Masters.

They were seated in a semicircular pattern, with one ancient-looking man in blue robes set before them on top of a cushion that placed him slightly elevated to the rest. There was an ominous looking vacant cushion set across from him. Kamala motioned me toward it.

I walked to my prescribed seat, and bowed before the old man, as Kamala instructed.

"Sit here," Choi Leung directed. His voice sounded ancient, as well. I sat down on the cushion and brought my legs quickly into the lotus position, remembering Deirdre and thinking how proud this simple act would have made her. Several Masters took note and smiled, including Kamala, now seated off to my left.

The top of the old man's head was bald, though long strands of gray-white hair fell in a braid down his back. His eyes were colorless, enveloped in a thick opaque film. Diabetes, Kamala would later explain. Choi Leung looked at me with those sightless eyes and pronounced to the others, "I sense within this vampiric form before me the wisdom light of the *Way* and an Adept of the Art of Slaying Vampires."

Murmurs arose from the Masters, and I saw some heads nodding while others were shaking in mixed response.

"Speak, my child," Choi Leung beckoned. "Let them hear for themselves the truth of your being."

"I don't really know what to say to all of you," I began. "I'm sitting here, in a vampire's body, but I won't kill. I was strongly compelled to at first, but I got myself through it."

"Is there no trace of bloodlust within you?" came a thick, French accent from the back. A Master with raven black hair.

"None," I replied.

"Not even out of some *curiosity*?"

"None," I repeated.

Then I heard a female voice amongst the Masters. I followed it back to locate a robed woman with a serene face and a shaved head; the only female present. This Master said, "We understand that in your time of crisis you repeated a mantra. What mantra was it, please?"

"Om Mani Padme Hum," I replied.

"Fascinating," came a voice from behind me.

And the woman continued, "Who gave you this mantra? Were you involved in study with a Master previous to your transformation?"

I gave her a solemn stare. "It was given to me by a young woman ... She was a student of this thing you call the *Way*." I paused in painful remembrance of the alleyway. "She's gone now. We were murdered together. And I was ... trapped, in this cage that's sitting here in front of you. I've tried to commit suicide, to escape, to get to out somehow ... but I've always failed. And then last night I followed another vampire into Carmilla's Kitchen to find some way to release myself. I didn't have time to find out if they could help me. Can you people help me? I offer you anything that you believe I can give in return."

"An equitable trade," commented Choi Leung. "Now tell me. What did you find in this place called Carmilla's Kitchen?"

At this Choi Leung looked to Kamala for clarification.

"A Den that we had discovered. It was raked last night by a team of agents led by one of my students, a third-level Initiate named Garett."

"They believed I was one of them," I began. "I spoke with a vampire who had had his eyes and mouth sewn shut."

"A strigoi," murmured the Frenchman. "He must have crawled out of the woodwork."

"He told me he made it his business to know each Dark Brother who entered the city."

"Dark Brother," whispered Choi Leung. "Here is a term that I have never heard used before. Have any of you heard this term?"

No Master present had heard it.

"Well," he began again. "I can already see your grand worth in the scheme of things. How now could any of us possibly learn such a term as 'Dark Brother' from their lips? Such a simple and terrible phrase. A drop of insight into their ways. A remarkable piece of reconnaissance for us."

"Unfortunately, that's about as far as we got before your people broke in and started sticking stakes in them. I think he may have gotten away, or at least he was not killed by Garett's men inside. I saw him make his way out the same way that I did."

"How else *killed* than by Garett's men?" Choi Leung asked.

"I don't know. What I meant was that maybe he'd been one of the vampires slain by the Master outside on the street."

"A Master was present?" Choi Leung asked Kamala. "I was not informed that a Master was present. Whom?"

At this Kamala gave a bewildered shrug. "To my knowledge, there was no Master present during the mission."

Choi Leung mirrored Kamala's bewilderment and asked, "Who was this Master you speak of, and why do you call him a Master? How did you recognize him as such?"

"By his radiance," I told him, confused how these people

could have lost track of one of their own. "He had the same lights about him as all of you ..."

"You see lights about us, do you?" he interrupted. "Amazing. What did this Master do? Did he communicate with you in any way?"

"Yes," I replied. The slight acceleration of Choi Leung's heart rate made me aware for the first time that indeed there was a human being sat across from me. A very wise, yet frail human being. The heart that pumped life through this man was not healthy; I could hear it so clearly. I felt within him a mastery over that heart rate, a mastery over his breathing that seemed almost greater than human capacity. But just as he'd asked me that question—his heart skipped several beats. "Yes, he delivered quite a speech to me there in front of the bar, with the ashes of seven vampires around him."

"Perhaps a rogue?" one of the Masters inquired of Kamala. "But why not make contact with your team?"

"Perhaps," replied Kamala, perplexed. "Perhaps he was otherwise tasked. Perhaps he considered our friend here of greater importance. Perhaps he is making that contact now."

"What speech?" Choi Leung demanded of me. "What message?"

I strove to remember the words of the message, precisely. As they seemed of paramount importance to these people. "He said something like this ... I deliver to you a message, Gentle One. That's what he called me. Then he said ... I had his blessings and shouldn't kill myself. That the things I had learned would, I think he said something like ... bode well for all things. That the changes that I perceived as accidents were not accidents. That the turns of my life had been inspired by this course, and that I should follow it. And that I should seek to teach the lessons that I've unlearned."

No one spoke for a time. Choi Leung brought his body back under control. I believe he garnered information from my pronouncement that he never fully shared with me. He seemed to regard me, though, in a strange new light. I thought it might be a good time to begin a line of questioning of my own.

"Why the wooden stakes?" I asked. "What power is there?"

To which he replied, "Stakes of Atonement. Sacred wood. Wood from the Aspen tree. Wood from the tree from whose branch would bear the weight of Jesus Christ, the Enlightened."

I was taken aback. "You're all Christians then?"

To which Choi Leung replied, smiling, "Not as you may think, but yes, we do believe in the teachings of Jesus of Nazareth. Each of us follows the *Way* on a path of our own devising. We seek to uncover the truth within ourselves. Christ is just one step on that path, as was Gautama, or Moses, or Mohammad. All of them living embodiments of the *Way*."

A biblical verse came then to mind that my father once read to us at Thanksgiving, from the book of St. John. It went, *"I am the way, the truth, and the life: no man cometh unto the Father, but by me."*

"Many religions," Choi Leung continued, "just as there may be several sides to the man. Religions are made of strict doctrines, some of which may be profoundly lucid expressions of truth and compassion, which ultimately lead to the *Way*. But they are only steps, not the *Way* itself."

"Yes," I told him. "I understand what you're saying."

"Tell him," injected Kamala, "of the young one you slew in the park."

"I didn't slay that kid ... he just *blew up!*" I answered. "I still don't understand how it happened."

"Due to your intervention?" Kamala inquired, prodding me.

"I don't understand the question."

"Do you believe that vampire would have destroyed himself had he not encountered you?"

"How can I know that?"

"Indeed, how can you not?"

"The *how* is not paramount here," Choi Leung stated, flatly. "You *are* a slayer of vampires. These lights you see about us, are about you as well. This inquiry has but one final question before we disperse. What are your intentions?"

"There is further knowledge that I require, Sir," I proposed modestly. "I believe your Ministry has that knowledge. I'm asking you for your help and I offer my services, whatever you feel they may be, in return. I'll have my answers, Sir. But if you can't help me, then I guess I'll be forced to seek *them* out again."

"Well said," he replied. "The truth at all cost. Very well, I accept you within the confines of this monastery, for as long as you may abide by its rules. In return, I ask only that you share knowledge freely with my disciples. To teach them in any fashion they may require."

"But I am no teacher, Choi Leung."

"Is that so?" he replied with a grin. "We shall see."

11

S eek to teach the lessons you've unlearned," paved the path I then followed, teaching them what I had become and learning that my life could still have a purpose.

Choi Leung decided that my greatest instruction would come through my step-by-step interactions with his disciples, as they rose through their successive training levels.

I began sitting at all evening meals with the Aspirants, learning their trials; the questions (called *koans*) the Master had tasked them to answer, as they strove towards their first *satori*.

First though, I had to negotiate their initial loathing of me.

"We are learning to kill the likes of you," came an arrogant voice during one introduction. "So, why do you keep trying to be our friend?"

That hurt. I wanted to grab him by his robe and drag him across the table, but I took a deep breath instead. "No, I believe you are mistaken, my brother disciple," I began, as the blood drained away from his face. "You're not here to learn how to kill. You're here to learn how to protect life at all costs. I hate them for what they've done to me more than I pray you should ever know. I'm here to help you learn how to stop the killing. So, whether you happen to like me or not doesn't matter to me at all. But I think you should get your facts straight, and maybe rethink your purpose for being here."

From that point on, all the Aspirants, including that one, grew friendly with me, and some of them would come and sit with me after evening meals in the small garden behind the kitchen, where I often came to meditate.

I took to wearing one of their monastic robes, called *kesas,* instead of my street clothes, as I found the soft cotton quite comfortable against my overly-sensitive skin. Eventually, I quit wearing shoes on the grounds.

I watched as the disciples, each in turn, swore their vows to the Four Noble Truths and the Eightfold Path; though I was not permitted to attend any weapon presentations, as these were strictly private affairs. Speaking with Choi Leung on the subject, he suggested the time was past due that I should receive one myself.

With some trepidation, I accepted.

It was the very first time in the sect's recorded history, of which I had become a devout student, that a Stake of Atonement had been placed in the hand of any man who had not made his vows of service and pronounced the dissolution of his former life. Or into the hands of a vampire, for that matter. But Choi Leung had tasked himself with transforming me into a teacher of the *Way,* with or without my consent, and he saw my attainment of complete understanding of all aspects of this monastic life as an essential step toward that goal. Besides, he was convinced that somewhere, somehow, I had already sworn those same vows which were sworn by his disciples. The Ministry concurred fully, for any damage that I might inflict back upon them would not be multiplied or diminished by the loss of one Stake of Atonement. Besides, according to the case studies I'd read, quite a few had already been lost.

To actually hold one of the things in my hand, though, engraved with my own grip, that was a little overwhelming at first. I saw it with the stark irony of handing a pack of matches to a drunken pyromaniac who has just finished dowsing himself with gasoline and saying, "Here you go, take these matches and try not to get yourself in any trouble, okay?"

As far as any inherent power within the wood itself, I felt none. Choi Leung seemed to read the disappointment on my face at the lack of revelation I received from holding the Stake. It made him rather giddy.

I held the thing up to my breast and asked, "What would happen if I were to be impaled with one of these? Should I try?"

His reply was a hearty good laugh, and never a word more. Personally, I don't think he had any real answer for what would happen, but his response was appropriate in lieu of what he saw in me as childlike fascination.

So, Stake in hand, I aspired toward the next step amongst the disciples—attainment of the killing ground. I found that each step came much easier for me than for the others. Several disciples, wishing to spend time in practice along-side me, received permission to reschedule their meditation and sleep periods, in order to train with me by night.

I learned to cast my physical awareness a good three feet away from my body, the ease of which I attributed to the state of misalignment that I felt already existed between my consciousness and this nocturnal shell that my body had formed.

"STRIKE! HIT! GO! STRIKE AGAIN! DO NOT THINK! STRIKE!" came the Master's demand of his disciples, as if therein lay the only vocabulary that made sense. "DROP AWAY FROM YOUR BODY OR ONE DAY SOME VAMPIRE WILL TEAR YOU TO PIECES!"

The students became so obsessed that they struck while they ate, and they struck while they pissed, and they struck as they sat in meditation.

For them, the training was different than it was for me, these fine young men and women, many of whom had lost loved ones to those they now sought to destroy. Different, because for them this training was just as the Master described, A MATTER OF LIFE AND DEATH!

So, I began spending less and less time in the practice hall, and longer and longer periods of time in my meditation. The Master Choi Leung, having become aware of my periods of communal absence, sought me out and found me sitting alone in my chamber one night. I remember looking up to him, standing in my doorway in his blind countenance, and expecting some form of reprimand; but instead, he merely sat himself down beside me, and fell into meditation.

We sat there together, in nothingness, for close to seven hours and then came his voice across the desolate landscape. "Morning is coming, my friend. Need you not sleep?"

"Perhaps not," I replied. "Why not seal yourself in here with me and we'll find out what happens?"

"Done!"

And we sat and we sat. It lasted for three full days and

just under four nights, during which time we both made
satori.

As we came out of it, he smiled and said, "Sir, I am
hungry."

Both of us felt we had learned something from our
shared meditation, but the Master refused to yield his information until he had eaten. We were suddenly like two children, sticking our tongues out at each other across the
dining hall table. I watched him patiently as he ate at his
soup and sipped his tea.

"Very well, then," I said after a time. "I wish to take your
Blackened Gate. I wish to take it immediately."

"As you wish," he replied between a chuckle and a sip.
"You shall be granted a period of twenty-four hours in which
to ..."

"No twenty-four hours, Choi Leung. I'm ready right
now."

"Indeed."

IT TOOK several hours for the Ministry men to arrive on the
grounds with the cargo that Choi Leung requested. As the
van pulled in under cover of darkness, it passed quite near to
the grove where I waited. Perhaps it was just my imagination
running wild, but I was sure at the time I could hear the
sounds of someone banging like mad from inside of the
cargo hull. My Blackened Gate, no doubt.

I felt someone approaching behind me, and turned to
find Garett, the Ministry agent to whom I'd surrendered.
The jacket and jeans now replaced with a *kesa* resembling
my own, with insignia denoting his rank.

"Evening," he said. "Mind if I join you?"

To which I replied in the monastic lingo, "Your presence is most graciously sought." And then, "Nice to see you, Garett. How's hunting?"

"Too good," he replied. "I think we're on the brink of a Black Season."

"I'm not familiar with the term."

At this he sat down in the grass and motioned me to sit. "We're not sure exactly when or why," he began after a time. "But they seem to follow some lunar cycle to breed more of their kind. If we don't track it and halt it correctly, the breeding can get out of hand. To the point where there aren't enough Stakes to go 'round. That's what we call a Black Season."

"How often?"

"Like I said, we don't know. Last one was nine years ago. That's when I got these." And he showed me his bare arms, which had parallel scars running their length. "Meat was torn down to the bone. Lot of physical therapy. I was still a rookie. Last one before that was thirty-one years ago, and that one was global. Lost Minsk, Jakarta, and nearly lost Paris before we finally got it under control. And mind you, in that time there were twice the amount of Masters roaming about. Right now, the Ministry is young again, and young is dangerous."

"Can I be of any help?"

"Depends."

"On?"

"On whether or not you slay vampires, my friend."

"Well then," I said with a handclasp to his shoulder. "Isn't that what we're about to find out?"

We got up and walked to the rear entrance of the zendo. "What have you brought for me?"

"Really wild SOB. Hell's Angel. Tough mother."

"Fine," I said. "That sounds fine."

"Oh," he said, scratching the back of his head. "There's one other thing. The Ministry requested we get this on film. If that's all right with you?"

At that I had to laugh. Of course, they would want this event recorded. Vampire versus vampire to the death—how spectacular.

"Fine with me," I answered.

We reached the rear entrance and he pulled the screen open for me. "Just out of curiosity," Garett asked then, "you nervous?"

"Nah," I replied. "What's he going to do, kill me?"

———

IT WAS a chamber in the monastery to which I had never been permitted entry, and yet I experienced a near-overwhelming sense of *déjà vu* as I came through the door. Choi Leung was the first face I saw, and that smile still hung on his lips. Beside him were two Masters I had not seen before, adorned in gray robes. Their conversation halted abruptly as I walked in.

In the center of the room was a large stone slab which I knew would lead down to the pit where the confrontation would take place. "I'll be up here filming," Garett whispered. "Unless you tell me otherwise. You have every right."

"No," I whispered back. "You go right ahead."

Several mantras were chanted by Choi Leung himself, and at the conclusion he added, "Here we defile the sanctity of the practice we know as the Blackened Gate. We do so in the interests of science, with the hope that the knowledge we gain today shall come to benefit all of Mankind. Proceed."

The stone slab was moved, revealing the dark subterranean chamber.

They moved to lower me down and I waved them away.

"No Stake," Garett cried out. "He's unarmed!"

And I leapt down into the pit.

The stench was awful. Vampires had been slain here. Humans had been slain here. I suddenly regarded the entire test as barbaric. I heard Garett switch the camera on high up above me, and then there came the low drone of the film clicking off on its spools.

I closed my eyes and whispered softly, "Om Mani Padme Hum. Om Mani Padme Hum. Come on. Come on!"

A stone moved that was set in the wall opposite me, and I saw two Ministry men force the vampire into the pit, releasing his binders as they shoved him forward. Then they sealed back the opening.

He was big, still dressed in the blood-soaked garb of a Hell's Angel, with a fanged jaw that protruded farther than any jaw I'd ever seen. He was riled, hungry and scared, and he wanted out of there. I felt for him. But then I thought, *this is a killer of innocent men, women, and children!*

Then he came at me with a ferocity and speed that I hadn't expected. I heard Garett above me whisper, *"Oh, shit!"*

He slammed into me hard and sent both of us careening into a roughhewn stone wall. Before I could react, he reached out with his right hand and clawed a deep gash across my chest, before quickly backing off.

The wound was opened and visible through the rag he had made of my kesa. But no blood came.

The beast was shaken at this.

He knows I'm not human! Perhaps I can reason with him?

"Look," I said. "You don't have to die here. See me? You could become like I am. You won't ever have to drink blood from ..."

Again, the brute lunged forward, madness in his eyes, and as I sidestepped him my hand snapped out, reflexively. Will of the killing ground.

It snapped out with a will all its own. Striking his chest in the kill zone. Striking true.

But there was no Stake.

He cried out in pain and spun floorward, collapsing into a heap.

I looked down and I saw that again his claws had found me, and a large gash had been scored down my left leg, leaving tendons exposed. "Listen to me," I screamed then, as he rose. "You can change! I swear you can! See me and know that the killing can end here and now!"

He came at me again, and again my hand slashed forwards in a tight arc and struck his chest. This time though, he managed to cling on to me and maneuver his body behind me, wrenching my back muscles and firmly pinning my arms to my sides.

Then his teeth went in me at the throat.

"There is nothing there for you," I yelled. *"You've already seen to that!"*

I squirmed against him, freeing an elbow and driving it into his stomach with all of my strength. He went slamming back hard against the wall, groping after me. Then I turned on him quickly, and he suddenly froze. All at once, the ferocity seemed to drain out of him, just as it had for the boy in the park.

The vampire sagged against the wall, slid down to his knees.

I heard Garett leap down into the pit, then move up behind me until we were shoulder to shoulder, the camera still running.

The vampire looked up to me, confused, *You have no blood, how can you be?*

Then he turned his attention to Garett, and a wave of revulsion washed over him. He retreated on all fours back against the wall until he cornered himself, unable to back away further. He looked down at his own gnarled hands, seemed to study them, as if he did not expect them to move under his control. "These ain't *my* hands!" he whispered aloud.

Then reached up and started to claw his own face with those hands and screamed, "NO-NO-NO-NO-NO-NO-NO!"

He gouged his own eyes out, right there in front of us. Then suddenly burst into flames.

I turned and climbed out of the pit, as Garett continued his filming.

Choi Leung stood waiting, fingers steepled beneath his chin, deep in contemplation.

"This is what I have learned, Master Leung," I told him. "That I *am* a Stake of Atonement."

"It is so," he replied. "But you are much more than that."

Garett came back up through the hole, and kept the camera rolling.

"It has dawned on me from the first, and now makes itself clear," he began, in a prophetic voice that echoed around the chamber. "That surely you have lived here, and completed this training before. Welcome home."

I was speechless.

THE UNIVERSE, the world, the *Way*, the moon, the menses, and this life that I was leading were all supposedly moving in cycles within cycles. In Buddhism they call it the wheel of *Karma*, a nature of the *Way* which whirls us through a multitude of lessons and rebirths in order to bring us closer and closer to the target of self-actualization.

Now, amusing yourself by thinking about reincarnation and how some screw up in a former life could now be affecting you in your present life is one thing. Having a Zen Master tell you to your face that this is so, is quite another.

Could it be true? I searched for some answers within myself. *Could I have been here before? Could I have "Lived" before? And if so, what evil could I have possibly done to deserve now this curse into Vampiredom?*

These are the questions that ran barking through my mind like wild dogs as the helicopter began its ascent from the grounds of the monastery. Choi Leung and his disciples had seen me off with fervent bows and handclasps. I waved goodbye to them until they seemed like specks on the terrain below us.

Only moments after Choi Leung's spectacular revelation as to my presumed origins, Garett had received urgent orders calling him back to the New York headquarters.

My Blackened Gate completed; I was obligated to leave.

So, I hitched a ride.

"What's your view on what Choi Leung said?" I had to shout to Garett, sitting barely two feet away, in order to make myself heard above the nonstop *chucka-chucka* of the chopper's props.

To which he yelled back, "Sure, why not? I'd be willing to

bet you were a Zen Master at least a couple a' times before now!"

"You think so?"

"Yeah," he said with a wink.

I must say I firmly admired this Ministry man. He fully embraced a system of beliefs that were based on intangible promises. There was a confidence that pervaded him, there as he sat staring out at the clouds, holding an undeveloped canister of film on his lap, which he felt could reveal the miraculous. An unshakable confidence.

Garett's leadership prowess was legend, and I'd read the file that detailed his promotions up through the ranks to his current position as Assault Team Commander. His slay ratio wasn't the highest for his region, although it was close, but his hostage survival rate stood unmatched worldwide. I wanted to learn what this man was about. I wanted to know what he felt in his heart when he slew.

Soon the Manhattan skyline came into view, and soon thereafter we were threading our way through her skyscrapers and beginning our descent.

"We're on final approach," the pilot called back. "Prepare to deploy."

I looked down as we came in low over Ministry Headquarters, and could make out several Ministry men whom I recognized, standing near the pad. "Sure beats driving in bound up in the trunk of a car!" I mused.

"Yeah, I'll bet!" he replied. "Think you'll ever forgive me for that?"

"Long forgiven," I said. "Besides, according to Choi Leung this has all been my idea, somehow."

12

The Vampire Sciences.

"There's no such thing as Spontaneous Human Combustion, my friend," said the thin, tight-faced man with an arrogant tone. "That's a term devised by charlatans and ignorant medicine men, who perhaps witnessed a Vampiric Combustion then chose to refer to it with their limited vocabulary and the barest minimum of observational skill. You sure as hell can't describe *your* kind's demise with such misinformed jargon. Makes me nauseous."

His name was Dr. Reginald P. Schrager, Ministry operative, expert Vampirologist, overbearing son of a bitch. The man had a chip on his shoulder when it came to me, and made no attempt to conceal it.

"They're not *my* kind," I said.

"Either your heart's beating or it's not," he replied. "You've got fangs or you don't. I realize you're not into sucking blood, and I respect that, but in the interests of science you're *un*dead, pal. You're a vampire."

"Yes," I snapped back. "And maybe you lost somebody to

someone who looked like me and it screwed you up. But it wasn't me, and you're starting to piss me off. If you don't quit it, I might just show you how much of a vampire I am!"

It had been a long night and was nearly sunrise.

I guess I touched a nerve in him, because from that night on he seemed able to tolerate my presence—in small doses. He taught me everything I know about blood, human and vampire, and the diseases that can infect the blood. Together, we used this knowledge to gain insight into my inability to commit suicide.

Once a human's blood has been ingested into a vampire's body it gets broken down at the molecular level and recombined with a highly volatile antigen that's flammable under certain conditions. We call the antigen VRh. When a vampire combusts, it's always due to VRh ignition. And, just as lighting a match requires three elements—oxygen, heat (in the form of friction), and fuel (paper or wood)—VRh requires three elements for ignition. Two are known and one remains unknown.

The first element is heat, found at extreme enough temperatures to break a vampire's skin and make direct contact with the VRh-infected blood, causing direct ignition. Indirect ignition can be triggered by contact with direct sunlight, the sunlight acting as a lifeforce supercharger, igniting the VRh blood as it penetrates a vampire's pores. It's like overcharging a lithium-ion battery until it explodes.

The second element is Aspen wood, which bears trace isotopes combined in a unique fashion that, accompanied by a small burst of oxygen when the Stake penetrates the vampire's flesh, creates friction resulting in VRh ignition.

Which brings us to the unknown ignition element. Various field accounts, and my recent Blackened Gate experience, suggest that vampires can somehow ignite their own blood by act of will—spontaneous combustion. We don't know how or why.

Dr. Schrager concluded that my inability to suicide was due to having no blood in my body. No fuel, no ignition. No blood, no combustion. No *life*, no *death*.

The Ministry leaders wanted to know whether I could be counted on to repeatedly trigger that third, unknown element in vampires. And if so, why and how. And, perhaps most important, could it be replicated or taught?

WHEN SCHRAGER and his associates weren't teaching me vampire physiology or running their various tests, Garett and his team were teaching me the rules of the Hunt.

The Ministry has any number of contacts (or *eyes*) scattered about the city, in the most unlikely places as well as the most public. There are *eyes* at all the colleges, and my first Hunt followed a report that came in around one in the morning from Columbia University, East Campus.

The alert found Garett, Craig, and me sitting in the recreation room watching one of our favorite movies, a garishly poor vampire film entitled *Jesse James Versus Dracula*, with such wonderful lines as, "Your six-guns are useless, Jesse, against the Powers of Darkness!"

We rushed immediately down to the parking garage where the vans were being prepped. Four Slayers on hand, myself included, in our van as the primary, and three in the backup unit that would patrol the surrounding area until Garett called them in. A cleanup unit would follow if necessary.

Everyone was equipped with walkie-talkies and multiple Stakes. The vans themselves were veritable warehouses of weaponry, explosives, climbing tack, and firefighting and fire-establishing gear. The Ministry was never lacking in the very latest and finest of all equipment.

The cleanup vans, which I had had less time to examine, were primarily used for either corpse removal (in a self-contained freezer) or corpse containment (in a stainless-steel cage).

Craig drove at breakneck speed, whipping in and out of light evening traffic on the Cross Bronx Expressway as Vivaldi's *Winter* played on the van's cassette recorder. Garett was tuned in to a headset and speaking directly with the *eyes* on campus. The third man, a Slayer called Danson, was strapping on body armor.

"What's the armor for, Danson?" I asked him.

He was a tall, muscular man in his mid-thirties, soft-spoken with dark, piercing eyes. Very straitlaced. He could have easily donned a suit and tie and worked on Wall Street. We'd only met recently, and he still wasn't sure he could trust me.

"I'm front man," he said. "Sometimes we get in and they're not even vamps, just thugs with guns. Hell, we went into a call once where it *was* a vamp with a machine gun. Remember that, Craig? Snyder took one in the gut."

"I remember," Craig said, spinning the van through a turn onto the West Side Highway. "I had to drag the fat bastard out of there."

"Hold up," Garett cut them off. "I'm getting coordinates. Craig, you know Columbia pretty well?"

"Yeah," Craig said. "Where are they?"

"Lowe Rotunda. Used to be the library."

"I know it."

"Take us around back; there're already cops on the scene."

"Got it."

We screeched onto the grounds and pulled up behind two NYPD cars and three security vehicles, lights blazing on and off like a beacon to every student on campus. People were streaming toward the spectacle in droves. Craig shut off the engine.

"Okay boys, let's stake 'em and rake 'em!" Danson shouted.

We slid out of the van and weaved our way through thronging students up the wide white marble steps to the building's entrance.

A disturbed police sergeant motioned us to stop.

"We're with the Ministry," Craig said.

"I don't care what church you're with, mister," the cop responded. "We've got a hostage situation and you ain't gettin' in."

He crossed his arms and gave Craig a defiant look. Garett was listening to orders through his headset.

"We've got no time for this, Craig," he said.

Craig decked the policeman with a hard left, and we went in. No sooner had we entered than we heard screaming somewhere above us.

"*Eyes* says third floor," Garett said. "Let's take those stairs. Danson, you're point. Craig, back us up."

Garett turned to me.

"You sense anything?"

I opened myself up as we mounted the stairs, took several deep breaths, and smelled vampires.

"There are definitely bloodsuckers here," I said.

We heard several shots and quickened our pace, coming out of the stairwell and taking up positions behind a set of closed double doors. Another shot rang out just beyond them, accompanied by more screams. The doors had framed glass decorative insets, perfect for viewing. Garett produced a palm-sized mirror and held it at an angle, to see into the room through the glass.

"These doors open onto a large hall," he whispered, slowly shifting the mirror and scanning the room. "About sixty by sixty, looks like some sort of art gallery. I see one, two, three ... make that four targets. I see corpses, and ten to fifteen hostages, sitting on the floor by the back wall, some wounded. There's a large glass window on the east wall, open. *Uh-oh.* I see two men in blue. That's where the gunshots came from. They're pinned down in the opposite corner; look pretty cut up. Get ready."

Garett handed the mirror to Craig and spoke into his headset.

"Team Two, I want you on the ground, east side with a catch team in two minutes. Copy? We're going in."

Danson flipped his Stake back and forth from hand to hand a few times while taking deep breaths. Craig studied the situation through the mirror. Satisfied, he pointed the mirror directly at me, palm outward, so that it reflected back my image.

"See yourself?" he whispered, then chuckled. "Just kidding."

"Cut the shit, Craig," Garett snapped. "Now listen. Danson in at point, break toward the hostages, take out the one guarding them as you go. Then position yourself between us and them."

"Check," Danson said, crouching low by the door.

"Craig, you've got the first one by the window."

"Check."

Garett turned to me.

"One for me and one for you, your target's the farthest away. Got it?"

"Check."

"I don't want any of them out of here and running loose on campus, got that? How copy, Team Two? Are you in position? Copy. Good hunting, gentlemen. On my signal. Three. Two. One. Go!"

Danson kicked the door wide and broke for the hostages at the far side of the hall. The panic-stricken students huddled together, some already bloody. The wounded police officers crouched down behind a makeshift barricade of desks as Craig entered just ahead of me at a run.

Everything seemed to shift into slow motion as I entered and tried to get a fix on my target, feeling the shadowy presence of Garett following in close on my heels. Danson lunged into the air toward his prey, a deformed creature with long jet-black hair and half its face burned away. Craig, Stake unsheathed, circled a male vampire holding a female student in front of him as a shield.

The remaining two vampires hurtled toward us in a blur of motion as another one who hadn't been accounted for emerged from behind a pillar. I decided to move for that one first, changing direction and hitting him hard in a dead run, slamming him back against the pillar, nearly losing my footing. He turned, slashed out at my face, catching me across my forehead and tearing skin.

Releasing to the killing ground, I crashed my palm against his chest. He screamed and fell away. I turned toward the others in time to see Garett stake his opponent in the heart so hard the point came through the corpse's back. It roared and burst into flames.

Danson was on the ground, not moving, his target nowhere in sight.

Craig still faced off with the one holding the girl as a shield. In a flash he feinted in, broke the vampire's grip, grabbed the hostage beneath the arms, and pitched her through an open window. I thought he'd lost his mind.

Out of nowhere a female vampire with stark white eyes came at me. I hit her three times in rapid succession. She shrieked and fell limp in my arms. I dropped her to the ground, scanning the room for more vampires, and saw Craig rip his Stake from the one he'd fought.

Suddenly one of the police officers behind Craig was up and aiming his gun at me, finger tensed on the trigger, looking horrified.

"Wait!" I yelled.

But the gun had already fired. Time slowed down. I saw the flash before I heard the blast, then felt the bullet tear into my chest and shatter out through my back. I fell down on one knee, more out of shock than injury. Garett ripped the gun from the cop's hand before he could fire again, and jammed it into his own belt.

I clutched at my wound and felt time start to move normally again. Craig stood by the window, looking down, expressionless.

Garett moved first to Danson, checked for a pulse at his neck, then came over to see if I was okay, helped me to stand, and called into his headset.

"Five targets down and clean. One Slayer critical but stable. Hostages secured. I need ambulances now! I repeat: one Slayer is critical."

Craig limped over to us.

"Danson?" he asked.

"Not good," Garett said. "But he's still got a shot if they get a damned medical unit up here."

"What about the one I sent out the window?"

"She made it; they caught her."

"Thank God," Craig said. "I didn't see any other way to clear her."

The hostages milled about in confusion, some working their way along the wall toward the exit, some stepping over fellow students' corpses. Garett turned to address them.

"Everyone try and get a grip on yourselves. The danger is past. You're all safe. You'll have one hell of a story to tell your classmates tomorrow. Probably get straight As in all your classes this semester, just for being here today. Take it easy."

The cop who shot me staggered into view, eyes wide.

"Who the hell are you people?" he said.

"The Ministry," I said. "Thanks for the bullet."

"Yeah, nice shot, Sherlock," Craig added. "We'll take it from here."

Danson lived, but would never return to active duty. He became yet another set of *eyes*—on Wall Street (go figure).

That was my first hunt.

13

Ascension through the Initiate levels toward Mastery of the Art is made through coupling a Disciple's dawning self-awareness with experiential growth.

As the number of vampires slain by the Initiate increases, comprehension blossoms, compassion deepens, and adherence to Right Action (the Eightfold Path) becomes ingrained. The Disciple embodies Right Action.

The first time you slay a vampire, you may experience revulsion, as if you've slain a fellow human. Perhaps your second kill provides a deeper understanding of your place in the divine plan as a protector of the weak. Your twenty-fifth kill could reveal you as an angel of mercy to those trapped in an ongoing cycle of violence and negative action. And so on, until you rise above even the contemplation of such motives and purposes.

There comes a point at which a vampire appears, and *flash* the Stake has slain him with no lag between the target's appearance and its removal, and you find you have become but an instrument of the *Way*.

EACH SUCCESSIVE HUNT, I believed, brought me closer to mastery. I learned how vampires moved through the world cloaked by darkness, driven by bloodlust in a never-ending cycle of murder and human enslavement. I learned how to second-guess them, their choice of lairs, their predilection for certain types of victim.

I learned all the detection techniques the Ministry had to offer, and helped them enhance most of them. Quickly I became one of the Ministry's top operatives. I was rapturous in my duty, for now I had purpose and vested my salvation in that purpose. With each vampire I slew, I was saving the lives of countless human beings. That was as far ahead as I reasoned. Garett and Craig spent long hours into the night with me, debating our role in the universal scheme of things.

On occasion, I sat in meditation with the Master of Masters, or lectured his students, honoring my vow. The last time, Choi Leung tried to convince me again I'd walked among these gardens before.

"Why do you resist the idea of reincarnation?" he asked.

I had no response.

NEW YORK WAS UNDER CONTROL, or so we assured ourselves, as now our *eyes* were reporting in less and less. Vampiric incidence fell sharply. Months passed; we spent our nights playing cards. Kamala loaned out our teams' services to the surrounding districts, where incidence seemed higher than ever. We welcomed the chance to travel. Any team we merged with received us with almost celebrity status, in most cases deferring to Garett's leadership, even in situations where it was unwarranted. Garett always accepted the mantle of leader graciously, but I could see in his eyes this was no gift.

"I don't like it," he confided in me once while we linked with a team in Boston. "Not my city, not my territory, not my place."

The Boston team had their own impressive stats, so we stood by when they raked a small den in Cambridge. Garett was more than happy to stay out of the direct action. Craig seemed antsy, performing his Stake-twirling trick as we sat in our van.

"Maybe you need a desk job," Craig teased Garett. "You're starting to go a little gray."

Garett just smiled, a smile displaying the radiance of enlightenment. I realized he was approaching Mastery, and wondered how Craig understood this. How was I understanding?

When the Boston team moved into cleanup mode I asked permission to examine the corpses in their van. One of the freezers held the body of a young man in his late teens packed in ice, flesh blue, throat torn. Such a waste. His eyes were still open. I closed them, checked his earlobes. The right lobe was clear. But there it was on the left lobe.

I got Garett, brought him into the van, and slid the door closed behind us.

"Remember that hunt in Philly where I was sent down alone? I found a peculiar marking on a young girl who'd been a willing feeder. A black spider on the left earlobe."

I showed Garett the boy's earlobe.

"Perfect match. What do you think?"

"I'm not sure," Garett said, clearly troubled. "Same markings on two feeders. One in Philly and one way up here. Seems unlikely, unless there's some den-to-den infrastructure forming. Some kind of networking."

We let that roll around in our heads. Vampires for the most part are loners, like timber wolves, though at times they gather in covens of half a dozen or so for safety. In larger groups they get sloppy and pretty soon attract our *eyes'* attention, as they'd done at Carmilla's Kitchen. They seem unable to stand one another's company for long. The strongest vampires pillage the lifeforce from the weaker ones. They fight over territory. Things of that nature.

The spider tattoos at such great distance suggested unity of some sort. If they were organized, it meant danger ahead.

"This could be bad," Garett said. "*Real* bad. Let's keep this quiet for now. I need to talk with Kamala, as soon as we're back in New York."

14

Vampires are sentient beings, quite capable of rational and even transcendental thought once the pain and delusion of bloodlust has been satiated. I think that too many Masters neglect to explain this to their disciples.

Imagine you're a civilian, walking home from a party down a deserted street late at night. You're full, you're happy, maybe a little drunk. Life's moving along nicely. Suddenly around the corner springs Mr. Death. He doesn't care if you're a doctor, a lawyer, a hooker, or a checkout clerk at Macy's. To a vampire you're food. He sees only the blood coursing through your veins, your lifeforce he must drain to continue living. You can't reason with him. You can't tell him your grandmother loves you and you're in the middle of a great book. You can't outrun him or outfight him or even pay him a million dollars to pass you by.

He's going to feed off you, and that's that, because, truth to be told he can't see you. Not the sentient *You* that's inside you.

Vampires can torture humans without remorse because they've forgotten they were human themselves once. Some can never be satiated, believing if they can swallow enough blood, just a little more than the night before, they'll be able to contain it and end their pain.

Understand who it is that you're slaying.

Tragically fucked-up lost souls.

The Slayer who forgets vampires were once human risks becoming no better than they are, a killing machine. Slaying must be an act of kindness, liberating a fellow sentient being from its sickly existence, ending its suffering—a state of awareness and heightened responsibility, crucial to advancing in the Slayer's Art.

When you Stake one of them, think to yourself, *I am liberating this sentient being! I am putting an end to his suffering!*

I, who should have been aware of these things from the beginning, found this a most painful lesson. I still had a lot to learn—about myself and blood's transcendental nature.

———

THE MARK of the spider turned out to be worse than we'd feared, much worse. Reports spewed across the network in response to our inquiry. Spider tattoo in Sweden, spider tattoo in Shanghai, spider tattoo in Jerusalem—a tremendous vampire underground communicating on a global scale, to what lengths we could hardly speculate.

This new information ran like a cold shock up the Ministry's collective spine.

"I want to go in," I told Kamala. "I can infiltrate."

It seemed to me the greatest gift I could offer the

Ministry, a task only I could perform with a risk which was far outweighed by the chance to gain much needed reconnaissance. I could move freely among *them* and learn if the season was on the brink of a turn.

A convened circle of Ministry Masters disagreed, deeming me too precious an asset to gamble, saying the situation required further meditation before any action could be taken. Choi Leung, who'd stepped down as Council Chair, sent a cable indicating his agreement with the decision. Kamala also agreed, binding Garett, through their ties, to hold the same opinion.

But I couldn't be swayed from the course I'd already chosen, and it was then that I sought out Craig.

"You're damned straight, I'm in," came his unhesitant response. "I'm your backup."

———

GREENWICH VILLAGE HAS ALWAYS BEEN a black market for vampires, with its plethora of counterculture, New Age religions, and dark angel wannabes. It's one of those hot spots found throughout America that acts as a magnet to every lost poet, black hole, or teenage runaway, a place where vampires can walk the streets openly and draw no real attention. Just about everyone dresses in black and exudes the vampire image: dead during the day and alive by night.

"Hard to pick a vampire out in this crowd," Craig joked as we strolled down St. Marks Place. "Why do you suppose these kids all dress in black?"

"Maybe they're in mourning."

I scanned the crowd for the real thing.

"Mourning for what?"

"Who knows? But it must be important to affect so many. Know thine enemy, know thyself."

"Maybe. As long as it's not to know and then become thine enemy."

He stopped and indicated an entranceway.

"This place is on our list."

We walked down three steps from street level into the Lair of the White Worm. The bar was packed. A live band played acid rock, overtaxing their amplifiers. Smoke filled the air, mostly from cigarettes, some from pot. We sat at the bar. Craig ordered two beers.

I looked around, detecting no *un*dead. A woman and three men occupied a booth across from us—all junkies and obviously under the influence. I could count the track marks on the men's bare arms. The girl's eyes were bloodshot, fully constricted, set within blackened sockets sunk deep from junk. What a sorry lot.

Craig followed my gaze.

"Wondering that these are the people we fight for?" he said, seeming to read my mind. "Remember the teaching: sacrifice even your own liberation until all sentient beings are free from suffering."

"Of course."

"Fuckin'-A right. Sometimes I forget, too, when I see people like that."

"Mind if I ask how old you were when you signed up?"

"Nineteen. One of them killed my sister. I saw it happen. Garett was on the case. He talked me through it, sent me to speak with Master Kei San. He told me about the Ministry and offered to train me. Said I reminded him of the legend of Rosukai."

"Which is?"

"Rosukai was a thief and street beggar in Osaka in the fifteenth century. One summer he was arrested and brought to the Chancellor, who'd received reports of vampires pillaging a border town. He ordered Rosukai to stop the onslaught."

"That makes no sense."

"Tell me about it. But this is a legend. You want the rest, or am I distracting you?"

"I can watch them and listen at the same time."

"Rosukai spit in the Chancellor's face, and was then beaten, tortured, and left in the street to die. That night hordes of vampires scourged Osaka and many nobles met their ends. When the vampires returned the next night, a transformed Rosukai was waiting at the city gate, holding one of the Twelve Chaste Stakes of Atonement. He slew all of them, then installed a beggar as Chancellor and disappeared."

"That still makes no sense."

"Think of it as a *koan*."

"Did you ever ask Master Kei San why you reminded him of the legend?"

"I thought it best not to. I told my parents I was headed to school in Montana then signed myself into the monastery. Passed the Blackened Gate in under three years and got transferred here."

"Ever think you made a bad choice?"

"Never. Slaying vampires and saving lives is all I'm about. No philosophy, just the religion."

"What about the future, a wife, maybe children?"

He smiled, shook his head as if he couldn't believe what I was asking.

"Slayers don't get married," he said. "It's not feasible.

Look at what we do. Policemen, firemen—they have dangerous jobs, they can get killed. But we walk out there looking for mortal combat. It's always a matter of life and death. Imagine me saying to my wife, 'I'm off to work now, honey. I'll try not to get my guts spilled. See you after sunrise.'"

"You've got a point," I said.

"Don't get me wrong," he said. "I've had plenty of girlfriends. I'm seeing someone now. But I'm married to the Ministry till death do us part."

The girl junky caught my eye. Something in her look triggered my internal alarms. I realized she knew what I am.

"Pay dirt," I whispered to Craig. "She's a feeder. I think I'm about to make contact."

She excused herself from the men and walked past me toward the restroom. I waited a moment before rising to follow her.

"Wish me luck, Craig," I said.

"Luck," he replied.

She led me to a private booth at the back.

"I'm Sylvia," she said, indicating I should sit then sitting beside me. "Want a little give-and-take?"

"Have any interesting tattoos?" I said.

She smiled, pulled back her earlobe for inspection, then unclasped the first two buttons of her blouse, allowing me easier access. I noted a set of partially healed puncture wounds thick with scar tissue.

"What's the give?" I said.

I knew it was a suspicious question but couldn't think of a more tactful way to ask. She seemed eager to tell me about it.

"The give is the blood you give me back," she said, as if it were perfectly normal behavior. "I haven't had a blood fix in ages. Last time, me and Harry got so high we were able to lift our car by the bumpers. Harry's dead now. He was my connection. Now I can't even get into the parties. You'll help me out, right?"

She leaned in tight against me, placing her arms about my neck in anticipation, *expecting* me to drink from her and "give" back her blood.

"You *want* to be a vampire?" I said.

"Don't tease me," she whispered, nuzzling her mouth to my neck. "I just want a little taste."

It was true, by The Twelve, it was true—this young woman *wanted* to become one of *them*. And she clearly believed that even a bit of soiled blood from me would empower her. It was a realization of the utmost revulsion for me, but I managed to keep my shock under control, to keep from grabbing her and shaking the shit out of her, screaming something like, "WHAT THE HELL'S WRONG WITH YOU! BEING LIKE THIS IS THE MOST FUCKED-UP THING EVER!"

But instead I asked, "You know about the parties?"

"There's a big one tonight," she said, snaking a hand down my shirt. "Can you get me in?"

"Maybe. Where's it at?"

"Corner of Church and Canal in Tribeca. Big brownstone, in the basement."

"Thanks," I said, pushing her off me and rising.

She looked up, desperate.

"Aren't you going to take? Aren't you *going to give?*"

"I'm dry," I said. "Nothing to give."

"*Please,*" she pleaded, tears welling up in her sunken eyes. "I'll do anything."

I reached out and laid my hand gently across her heart, sending warmth (to what end I know not).

"I'm afraid that's the best I can do," I said.

15

Initiations.

The gulf between discipleship and mastery is enormous and building the bridge is often a lifelong task, more often than not an unrealized goal. A Master resides in a continuous state of pure action and motive. How many can claim this? Average men and women on the street? Perhaps one in a million. Monks and nuns living in monastic settings? A handful, at best. There have been moments of purity in my life, but I'm given to bouts of selfishness, pride, and egotism.

Comprehending my own lack of mastery affords me clearer insight into my colleagues' initiations. I've delighted when an Aspirant succeeds on the killing ground, to witness his awe as he realizes first contact with the mystical unknown. I've also seen Slayers with dozens of confirmed kills leave death sites in tears.

I believe each of us faces several key initiations that move us toward mastering the Art within. The trick is recognizing what initiation you're undergoing and making a conscious choice in that moment to ascend to the next level.

Every initiation I've witnessed has been in the form of some event that left the individual either dead or transformed. Keeping to the *Way* as best you can during these initiations raises awareness and helps make enlightenment possible—always bearing in mind that every stairway leads down as well as up.

Not all initiations are positive or life-affirming. When you go where angels fear to tread, you may not walk out the same way you went in.

Indeed, neither Craig nor I would ever be the same after that party.

Craig slipped two small metallic cartridges about the size of a deck of cards from his knapsack and passed one to me.

"This is a tracer," he said. "Ever use one?"

"No."

He touched a black button on the side of the one he held.

"Press this button and you're broadcasting. This light will flash. Anything gets screwed up in there, signal me and I'll come running."

"Keep yourself safe out here," I said.

"Yeah," he said. "You go in there and have all the fun."

"Welcome," said the doorman, a fat, balding, sweat-stained man who seemed to know what things were about, indicating a service elevator to his left, a rusty, dilapidated piece of machinery. "Basement."

I pushed the button and the gates *clank-clanked* open. I stepped inside the cage, only slightly uneasy. There were two buttons on the panel, the lower marked BASEMENT, beside which some warped individual had scribbled in marker *Press this button and somebody dies!*

I hesitated then pressed the button. As the cage descended, I prepared to pass as one of them, calling up images of atrocities I'd witnessed in dens we'd raked, telling myself, *You're a killer, humans are food, think like a killer, move like a killer, speak like a killer.*

Loud industrial music throbbed outside the elevator as it touched down. The cage gates *clanked* open.

I stepped into a surprisingly elegant, wide-open space with high ceilings and stone floors, lit solely by candles; the vampires were like additional small flames to my sight. A rough head count indicated nearly a hundred milling about, which was unheard of, and twice as many humans. The scent of blood was thick. There was laughter, dancing, and the sounds of glasses clinking. It really was a party.

I moved about, surveying as I went, stopping to accept a wine glass full of blood from a human waiter's tray as he passed.

Bodies writhed together on the dance floor, many of them mixed couples. A female vampire in a long gray gown pressed close to her pale human partner and spun him about to the music. Blood trickled down his shirt.

In the center of the dance floor was an altar, draped in black velvet, with several vampires and one half-nude human female perched atop. The vampires appeared to be rubbing her down with some kind of oil; no hostage there. I tipped half my drink into a wastebasket when no one was looking.

At the far end of the hall was a bar, similar to the setup at Carmilla's Kitchen, where human barmaids offered their blood to the customers.

I passed an ornate-looking mirror and was comforted to see I reflected exactly like other vampires in the dim light.

I overheard bits of conversation.

"This is *nothing* compared to the gatherings."

"Alexis certainly can draw a crowd."

A crashing sound as a table with glasses was knocked over by two vampires slashing at each other, drawing blood. I'd never witnessed vampire combat before. One of them was dressed in a three-piece suit, the other in little more than rags. They tore each other to pieces with equal brutality.

A dark-suited vampire detached himself from the crowd and intervened, catching the one in rags by the throat and sending him sprawling a good six yards backward across the dance floor, where two militant-looking vampires grappled him up and hustled him out of the hall.

"Great fight, huh?" came a human voice to my left.

I turned to meet the gaze of the girl from the altar. She'd changed into a long white gown and had her hair in a French braid. She was quite striking.

"I've never met *you* before," she said, apparently anxious. "Do you have an invitation?"

"I'm a crasher," I said, feigning embarrassment, lest she sound some alarm. "I hope that's all right?"

Her anxious expression turned to a smile.

"Consider yourself invited. I'm Corinne. I'm dying tonight. This is my induction party."

"Congratulations," I said, raising my glass, outwardly smiling while inwardly gagging. "Welcome to the family, Dark Sister."

"Thank you."

"Pleasure's mine. And it's such a lovely space. Does it belong to you?"

"It belongs to Alexis," she said quietly, as if letting me in on a secret, and pointed to the vampire who'd broken up the fight, who seemed somehow familiar. "He's going to turn me. He loves me."

"How fortunate for you," I said.

"I know," she said dreamily. "I *feel* fortunate to become like you—the power, the eternity."

The eternal suffering, I wanted to warn her, but couldn't.

I saw Alexis staring at us contemplatively across the hall. I raised my glass to him, uneasy now, and turned back to the girl.

"Where's Alexis from?" I asked.

"He's Rumanian," she said proudly. "A strigoi. Almost two hundred fifty years old."

I realized Alexis was the vampire I'd spoken to at Carmilla's Kitchen. He'd escaped.

"See that dark-haired woman who just came up and kissed him?" Corinne said.

The woman in question glanced my way.

"Her name is Siobhan. She's from Malaysia, where they call vampires *langsuirs.* It's your lucky night. Here they come."

They were heading straight toward us. I had nowhere to run, and ducking back into the crowd from our current position would be next to impossible. I steeled myself for the encounter.

"Well, well, my Dark Brother," Alexis said. "How pleasant to see you again. Was it four years ago? In the den beneath Carmilla's Kitchen. I thought surely you'd been slain by those bastard monks."

"I imagined the same of you," I said.

"I just barely got through. How did you escape?"

"By killing my way out. How else?"

"How else indeed?" Siobhan remarked, her tone cutting.

I had my finger on the tracer button in my pocket but realized pressing it would only bring Craig down to get wasted with me.

"You'll stay for the ceremony," Alexis said, offering no alternative. "Afterward we'll speak in depth."

He linked arms with Corinne.

"It's time," he said. Then, to Siobhan: "See that our guest remains attended, won't you, my pet?"

"Of course," she said.

All eyes, human and vampire, turned as Alexis led Corinne to the altar. Siobhan remained by my side, her arm resting gently on mine.

"Hark to the ritual, Children of Darkness," Alexis began, enthusiastic as any televangelist. "See before you this child of light, who by nature of the blood coursing through her veins, propelled by a beating heart, is herself the way of the light. See her and know that surely *we* shall inherit the Earth. In the Holy Bible, Old Testament, Leviticus chapter seventeen, verse eleven, the Lord God commanded, 'For the life of the flesh *is* in the blood: and I have given it to you on the altar to make an atonement for your souls: for it *is* the blood *that* maketh an atonement for the soul.' And so, we must drink to live. This young one wishes to shed her light and join us in our great penance of darkness. Through her sacrifice all of us are cleansed, my Dark Brethren. And she shall find her rewards in eternal life, eternal youth, eternal beauty—no longer a slave to the petty concerns of Man, empowered from a higher source, with a higher duty toward her former race. Forever forsaking the light of day to take up the divine post of Death Incarnate. A messenger of God. A mistress of life and death. A one-woman plague. A shepherdess to till the human fields of Earth. And so, we welcome this child of light as she becomes a child of night."

He bowed a moment in mock reverence for his own speech then turned and stretched his hand to Corinne, who moved slowly toward him, trembling.

Sentient beings of life, please aid this young one, I prayed silently.

"Do you give up your life for us, freely willing your soul to be born into darkness?" Alexis asked Corinne.

No! my soul cried.

"Yes," she said, her voice barely audible.

"And you understand that with your birth into darkness, you move mankind ever closer to divine grace with God?"

No!

"Yes."

The entire gathering stood on edge to the thrill of her pounding young heartbeat.

"Do you forever forsake the domain of Man, and the light of day, to ensure your sacrifice may benefit Mankind?"

No!

"Yes," she whispered.

Tears streamed down her cheeks as Alexis bent and sank his fangs into her neck, twisting her body around as if she were a rag doll. Her arms and legs flailed, fighting death, kicking, scratching, to the last drop desiring life.

I stood by, powerless, as a hundred vampires, all murderously envious, watched Alexis take her. I heard her final shuddering heartbeats, watched urine and excrement run down the back of her dress and puddle on the altar, eliciting a communal gasp from the assembled spectators. Every vampire present had known the tunnel, that glowing passageway Corinne now traversed. Each of us had felt that light denied and then returned.

Feeling the time approach, Alexis gouged the flesh above his own dead heart with his bare hand and hefted Corinne's mouth to his chest, to drink the oozing blood he'd stolen. Moments passed. There was no response. I rejoiced at the possibility he'd lost her. Then, barely perceptible, Corinne's tongue slithered over the red wound. Then again. Her body shuddered. Her back arched, forcing her mouth into tighter suction, her tongue working vigorously, her teeth digging.

She was dead, and she was going to live.

The assembled vampires drank with her—psychically—from Alexis. This strigoi was a fear the Ministry didn't know it should have, one of the rare few with the power of mass hypnosis. A true Prince of Darkness. Who knew to what ends he might use it?

Once Corinne was fully turned, Alexis lifted her into his arms and whisked her through a doorway behind the altar.

I needed to get the hell out of there. But how? First, I had to get rid of Siobhan—before Alexis returned. I could slay her easily enough, but not in the middle of everyone. How many vampires stood between me and the elevator, and how many could I take down before I was torn to pieces?

"Alexis is wondrous," Siobhan exclaimed. "Don't you agree?"

"Completely," I said, noticing the pendant hanging round her neck. A silver coin, engraved with the roman numerals XXX.

"Is there some meaning to your pendant?" I asked.

"It's a symbol of the children of Judas," she said. "Thirty

silver pieces was the price Iscariot was paid for selling Jesus. It's Rumanian. Alexis gave it to me."

"It's exquisite," I said. "May I?"

"Of course. Be aware: the numerals are sharp to the touch. Rumanian vampires used them to mark the flesh of their victims."

I reached out my hand and lifted the pendant from her breast, giving myself a clear shot and preparing to walk briskly but calmly toward the elevator.

Too late.

"I trust you enjoyed the ceremony?" came Alexis's deep vibrato behind me.

I let the pendant fall back on Siobhan's chest, and turned to him. Another vampire stood by his side, eyeing me up and down. He was young (or young when he'd died), late teens perhaps, his hair dark and long, hanging loose at his shoulders, his face flush from too much blood coursing through his body, visible also in his chest beneath his open shirt.

"Life's full of circles, my friend," Alexis said, grinning, then indicated the vampire by his side. "He claims to have made you."

Emotion pummeled me. I looked at him with unconcealed hatred.

"*You* turned me?"

"Yeah," he said, drunkenly. "Well, not exactly."

"Did you or did you not?" Alexis snapped, grasping him hard by the nape of the neck. "Speak the truth!"

"There were three of us," he said nervously. "We cornered him and his girlfriend in this alley, somewhere in SoHo. We took both of them out really quick 'cause the girl was a screamer. But you ... You just wouldn't stay down. You reached up and grabbed me. Yanked me to the ground. Bit down hard and took some back. I tried to beat you off me, but you were too fuckin' strong. You went crazy! The three of us tore out of there, you spooked us so bad!"

A tsunami of long-forgotten rage coursed through me. The killing ground reached out, taking control of my body, slamming my empty palm full force against his chest, dropping him hard.

"Deirdre," I choked out.

Alexis eyed me with curious indignation as he helped the vampire to his feet. The vampire studied his own hands, a passing waitress, Alexis, then looked at his reflection in the mirror.

"He's done something to me!" he screamed. "I can't take it!"

He burst into flames and was quickly incinerated.

"Very impressive," Alexis remarked, then turned and shouted, "Hold him! But mind the hands!"

Within moments four of them had grappled me to my knees. I tried to shake them loose and free my fists.

Alexis moved in close—so close, I could smell Corinne's blood in his mouth. He grasped my hair, yanked my head back, and pried opened my mouth to inspect my eyeteeth. I tried to bite down on his finger, and was rewarded with several hammer hits to the kidneys.

"You'll get nothing from me," I hissed.

His fingers probed my chest above my heart and lingered there.

"On the contrary, my Dark Brother," he said.

His hand moved over my abdomen. He looked perplexed. He slashed a hand across my face, slicing skin. No blood came. He searched my pockets and found the tracer.

"What happens if I press this button?" he asked.

I struggled to break free.

"Take him!" he ordered, indicating the back of the hall. As they dragged me off, I heard him call, "Search every nearby street! Catch the rats before they flee the sinking ship!"

I laughed out loud. My hysterics continued as they dragged me down a cement stairwell to a subbasement flooded with harsh, fluorescent light. I laughed in their faces when they lashed me to a chair with rusted chains and a steel collar for my neck—egging them on, certain they could do me no real harm.

Then they dragged Craig in and laid him on the floor. His left eye was little more than bloodied pulp. I could tell both his legs had been broken.

"You hang tough, Ministry man!" he called out.

Still I believed I had nothing to fear, that I could endure whatever damage they might inflict on me.

Alexis knelt down, pressing a knee hard on Craig's right arm. Craig looked at him with contempt, closing his eyes in pain as Alexis grasped his wrist and wrenched it forward, backward, then forward again until the hand and wrist were blue and just barely connected.

Craig remained silent.

Alexis went to work on his left wrist. When it was limp, he stopped, got up, and called for "the weapon." One of the vampires produced Craig's Stake from beneath his coat, handed it to Alexis. He studied it in the fluorescent light.

"The weeping wood," he said, rolling it between his hands. "The spoiled fruit of the Aspen, said to have been the wood of Christ's cross. On those trees we shall crucify any man who lifts this wood against us. We shall crucify your Ministry into a forest of the dead."

He placed the Stake on Craig's right hand, now unable to close, much less grasp it, and raised his own shirt, baring his chest.

"Place it here," he said mockingly. "What? Can't? Then perhaps you shouldn't be playing with such dangerous toys."

He set the Stake aside.

"Remove him," he ordered.

Craig didn't cry out as they dragged him from the room. I was proud of him. I wanted to follow his example and defy Alexis. I still saw no way they could harm me except exposing me to the sun.

Alexis interrupted my thoughts.

"You seem thirsty, my Dark Brother," he said. "Very thirsty."

"I'm not your brother, you rotten carcass!" I shouted.

"We'll see about that," he said. Then, to the others: "Bring me needles. Syringes. A girl off the street."

His dogs rushed to do his bidding.

———

THE FIRST NEEDLE went into my arm, forcing blood into my veins, burning through my body—slow, intoxicating. I struggled vainly to get out of the chair, chanting the mantra and trying to keep my eyes off the bound-and-gagged young blonde across from me, her face etched in horror, whose blood it was.

"Relax," Alexis told her. "You'll live through this. It's just a bit of blood for my friend here. His first taste."

The girl's beautiful green eyes flitted back and forth in terror from Alexis to me, her heart pounding like it might burst. I doubted she could understand what he was saying.

Damn Alexis. He had the power to hypnotize her into unconsciousness or feeling nothing. This torture was to add to my own. I prayed she'd faint or have a heart attack.

He turned to me.

"How exquisite to watch it rush through you. I can see how alive it's making you feel."

"*Om Mani Padme Hum. Om Mani Padme Hum. Om Mani Padme Hum.*"

My mouth and throat grew drier and drier.

"*Om Mani Padme Hum. Om Mani Padme Hum. Om Mani Padme Hum.*"

Alexis stuck the syringe in her again, this time just below her breast, pulled back the plunger to draw more blood.

"Take a little life ..." he said. She gasped as he plucked the needle free. A crimson stain dampened her blouse.

"And give a little life," he continued, as he stabbed the needle back into my arm and pumped it in me.

SEVERAL YEARS LATER, when this was all over, the curse finally lifted, I found my way back to the simplicity of New Mexico. I had left the Ministry, leaving them no forwarding address.

Things there were as I'd recalled, desert, mountains, friendly faces that could warm to strangers. I was just getting used to the inherent vitality of actually being *human* again. The feel of the sun on my face, the sound of my own heartbeat, the sight of my own blood whenever I accidentally injured myself. I was rediscovering life in all its simplistic wonder, and falling in love with the experience.

I was nervous as I walked up the paved footpath to the

entrance of the Crestwood Private Sanitarium. The automatic door swung wide. I went in, mouth dry, palms sweating.

"I'm here to see my sister," I told the sprightly young candy striper behind the reception desk.

"Sure," she said. "What's her name?"

"Chelsea Patterson."

"Wow," she said. "Chelsea talks about you all the time. Haven't you been away or something?"

"On business," I said.

"It's really great to meet you. You two look so much alike. She's in room three twenty-eight."

"Thanks," I said.

"No problem," she replied with a wink.

Too-bright fluorescent lights lined the ceilings of the long corridor. I hesitated at Chelsea's door. How would she receive me after all this time? Did she hate me for leaving her?

I knocked.

"Come in," her familiar voice answered.

Suddenly nauseous, I stifled a heave and opened the door.

She was lying in bed watching television. My scrawny little sister had blossomed into a beautiful woman. Her formerly straight blonde hair now draped in delicate curls around her face. Her blue eyes were clear and alert as she looked up at me.

"David!" she exclaimed.

She leapt from the bed, raced into my arms, and hugged me tight.

"Is it really you?" she said. "Have you come back for me? I was sure I'd never see you again."

My arms slid timidly across her shoulders, down to the small of her back as we embraced, her sweetness filling me.

I gently shifted her hair and sank my teeth in her neck—as Alexis plunged the needle into me for the third time, straight into my heart, and forced the plunger.

THE GIRL MOANED, and I opened my eyes.

Alexis was still pumping the third stream of blood into me.

"Who is this Chelsea?" he asked, withdrawing the needle. "Perhaps I can meet her sometime."

I felt my face flush for the first time in years as the girl's blood coursed through my system, raging silent war against the river of *Chi*. Thin blood-sweat began coating my body as my glands awakened. I was so high I could no longer distinguish the girl's features; her face blurred, becoming a reddish flame.

"Don't you bother about her, my Dark Brother. She's just a peasant. Given a choice, she'd see us both nailed down in our coffins and buried alive. Just think about how good her lovely blood makes you feel."

It *was* good. Ecstasy. It made me feel like I was human again. I wanted more. *Needed* more.

I conjured mental images of Choi Leung, Kamala, Garett, Deirdre, my friends, my teachers. It was no use. My body took to the blood like it was meant for it. In a way it was. It was the one thing that felt natural in my body's inherent unnaturalness.

"That should last you a while," Alexis said. "Please excuse me while I attend to your Ministry friend. We're going to have a lot of fun together. Feel free to call out to me if you must."

He started for the door then walked back to the girl.

"Scream for us a bit," he said.

THE THIRD DOSE engulfed me as he ripped off her gag. I shut my eyes against her wailing while her blood slithered its way through my long-dead veins. And once again I experienced the pain I'd finally overcome in the apartment—now fully awake, devouring.

Suddenly I was sitting across from Deputy Jones in that abandoned mill in Birchrunville, Pennsylvania.

"I'm bleeding to death," he said matter-of-factly.

"Yes," I said.

"Because of you and your blood-sucking kind."

He gurgled blood.

"No," I said. "I'm not like the others."

"Look at you," he retorted. "High as a kite."

"No, Jones," I insisted. "I didn't kill anybody. I never drank anyone's blood. This was forced into me. Do you understand the distinction?"

"I understand just fine. But I'm dying now. It would've been nice to get to know you better. Maybe I could've been one of your students. Now I'm dying and there's nothing you can do about it. So why don't you just slide on over here and take some of my blood while it's still warm? Don't be shy. I'm offering it to you."

I moved slowly toward him, my tongue gliding over my teeth.

The fourth needle went in, topping me off. Alexis pulled it out.

"That was quite a dose I just gave you. It should last you through the day. It's nearly sunrise outside. Your brothers are preparing a nice box for you. When you wake up tomorrow, you should have no need for further injections."

"What did you do to Craig?" I mumbled, barely coherent.

"Was that his name? I tortured him some more and then killed him, of course. Quite a distasteful mouth on him."

He moved to the girl, stroked her hair. He'd gagged her again.

"Tomorrow you'll be fit to kill, Dark Brother."

My body convulsed; shivers ran up my spine.

Two vampires came and locked me inside a pine box.

LYING inside a coffin until sunrise-induced sleep overtook me could have unhinged me had it not served as a physical barrier from the girl. That made the miserable claustrophobic experience just bearable. Her heartbeat drove me crazy, invading me, encompassing my thoughts, constantly drawing my attention. I was so high on her blood, I believed her heartbeat actually wanted to become my heartbeat, her lifeforce mine.

As the dose of her blood began waning, I felt the need in my system increasing in staggering disproportion. Every thought entering my head behind the backbeat of that youthful heart was like a cancer. If I told myself I could resist her, then almost instantly the pain struck. It was as if the pain itself was a sentient force that could spy out my thoughts and revenge itself upon me for threatening to starve it.

I thought of taking her, of satiating myself. The thought drove a stake through my sanity.

Thinking in either direction was like being slowly eaten alive. I knew I needed to stop thinking altogether, to rest in nothingness but, God help me, her presence out there was a madness I could not tune out of my head!

Thump-thump,   thump-thump,   thump-thump,   thump-thump ...

I tried chanting.

Om Mani Padme *PAIN!* Om Mani *PAIN-PAIN!* Om *PAIN-PAIN-PAIN! PAIN-PAIN-PAIN-PAIN!*

I opened my eyes and was standing in the middle of a dirt road. The sun, a half-remembered, warmly welcomed thing, hung high overhead. There appeared to be some sort of village in the distance. I knew it was a hallucination, and saw no way to escape it. But it was a welcome rest from the pain. I began walking toward the village.

On the side of the road an old man sat whittling a piece of wood in the shade of an Aspen tree. I walked up to him. He looked at me with a warm smile and enlightenment in his eyes.

"Please, sir," I said. "Are you a Master of the Art of Slaying Vampires?"

"I'm no Master," he said. "There is no such art. And there are no vampires."

"What are you making, then?" I asked, confused.

Clearly he was whittling a Stake of Atonement.

He held up the wood.

"This is merely a tent stake," he said. "Or maybe a doorstop. I haven't decided yet."

"Both useful," I said.

"Are you in trouble, my friend?" he asked. "Do you need help?"

"I'm in an hour of great need."

"And have you a master or teacher?"

"Yes," I replied. "Several."

"How fortunate for you. I see now you having nothing to worry about. Your master will sense your great need and shall come to your aid."

"You think so?"

"Yes."

"Please tell me, who are you?"

"Me?" He tapped a finger to his temple. "I was a fisherman once, and a prince, a mother, a father, a daughter, and a son. Once I was even a carnival man. Now I'm merely an image in your mind. Tell me, are you planning on heading into that village?"

"I'm not sure. What do you recommend?"

The old man smiled and held out the Stake.

"Take this," he said. "You might need it."

"I can't," I said, humbled.

"Take it," he repeated, holding it with the point toward his heart. "You'll need it. I can make more."

Compelled, I grasped the wood and felt my grip indent in the grain.

"Thank you," I said, looking up from the Stake.

The old man had vanished. I heard his reply in the wind.

"You are most welcome."

I headed for the village, the Stake slung by my side. The road grew barren as I got closer. By the time I reached the main gate, the sun had set. I entered the village in darkness, beneath a wooden sign reading *Welcome to Hell*.

I passed mud-brick dwellings with people inside watching me from behind doors and through windows. I paused at a movie theater, reminding myself anything is possible in a dream. Bright fluorescent bulbs lit up the marquee, forming words:

NOW SHOWING: FIGHTING THE BLUE DRAGON

There in my blood-fever dream I struggled to recall the reference to the Chinese fable. When a person suffers an affliction carrying him near the brink of death, he must descend into the earth's core to face the Blue Dragon, who holds the knowledge of all people's karma. The way is perilous. Within the Dragon's mouth rests a silver key. The dying man must find a way to retrieve this key, or he may never return to consciousness ...

I looked down at my hands, saw pulsing veins, and realized I was human again. I looked up. A dark-robed vampire at the end of the street stood blocking my path. He began walking toward me. I couldn't help but walk toward him.

At twenty paces, I reached down and brushed the Stake at my side, making sure it was still there.

At ten paces, I realized the vampire was me.

At five paces, he rushed at me.

The Stake flashed into my hand and buried itself in his chest. He dropped to his knees.

"Take this," he said with my voice.

He passed me a silver key. Blood gushed in torrents from his wound as I took it.

"Now wake up," he said, as a torrent of blood gushed away from the wound I had made in his chest. "Get up, go with them, and get out!"

Someone was shaking me vigorously by the shoulders. I couldn't open my eyes. I sensed it was still daylight outside, nearly dusk. I heard glass shattering and doors crashing inward. I smelled smoke.

"Wake up! We're raking the place. It's on fire."

I opened my eyes. It was Garett. Thank God.

I scanned the room. The lid to my coffin lay broken, discarded. The chair, where the girl had been bound, sat empty—a pool of blood beneath it.

"Craig?" Garett asked.

"The bastards killed him. I'm sorry. There was nothing I could do."

He was silent a moment.

"You don't look so good yourself."

"Blood in me," I confessed. "Get me the hell out of here."

16

W ithdrawal.

The *Way* itself should not be viewed as some alien religion, as too often is the case in Western thought. The *Way* is inherent in everything that is. It's already inside you, guiding you, trying to clear up your Karma. Unfortunately, there is also a great wild beast out there who is trying to trip you up with each step you take. That wild beast's name is *Samsara*. Its claws are ambition, its fangs are delusion, its lair is inside of your head.

Samsara is a word in Sanskrit that encompasses the realm of delusion in which the non-practitioner of the *Way* rests in his or her everyday life. Common man, especially in the West, spends the greatest quantity of time indulged in the most trivial of daily pursuits and passions and spends little to no time involved in any personal spiritual practice. I believe this is due in part to the way in which Westerners grow up with religion; complete with instructions and directives that seem to require no personal search, no incentive to seek out the truth for one's self.

Zen Masters know that their students cannot gain enlightenment by reading texts or from listening to even the most splendid orations. It's all about searching out truth from within. The only real difficulty in the task of seeking out this truth, which is already an indisputable part of you, is the sea of Samsara in which you are daily drowning.

Meditation, the study of Zen, is a tool used to buoy us out of this sea of delusion, and present the truth of the *Way* in its pristine, unobstructed form. To arrive at this state of clear seeing, this *emancipation of mind*, one must dedicate himself to a withdrawal from Samsara. Most people find great difficulty in trying to cast off this state of delusion while continuing to live in a world full of modern escapist technology. Many enter into some form of retreat or monastic environment for purification, as they painstakingly withdraw from illusions they fear had begun to define them. The stripping away of the fabric that you believe makes up your life can be quite painful.

Although, a Chinese Zen Master named Ekai, more commonly called Mumon, who died in the late thirteenth century, once commented:

The light of the eye is as a comet,
And Zen's activity is as lightning.
The sword that kills the man
Is the sword that saves the man.

GARETT SOMEHOW GOT me out of the den and home to the Ministry. I vaguely recall being hit by a burst of sunlight then stuffed in the back of a van. But if that actually happened, why wasn't I dead?

We sat in the medical center amid oxygen tanks and emergency burn care equipment. I lay under a heavy blanket, nude, my clothes having been removed at some point.

"Try to relax," Garett said, wiping the bloodsweat from my forehead while I shuddered.

My blood withdrawal alternately felt like it would set me on fire or shake me to pieces. I could still feel the blood in my mouth, my fingertips, my toes. It had a firm hold on what in life had been my central nervous system.

"Where's the girl?" I stammered.

"You kept asking me that on the way. There was no girl when we raked the place."

"It's her blood," I said, struggling to keep my eyes from rolling back in my head in pain. "If you hadn't gotten me out, I might have torn her to pieces."

"Nice guy like you? I doubt it," he said, grinning.

"Feels like I'm gonna shake to death," I said.

"Nah," he said. "Everybody's working on ways to patch you up. Let me ring the doc, tell him you're starting to make sense again."

I reached a trembling hand to touch him.

"I didn't kill anyone, Garett."

"I know that," he said.

He went to the phone on the wall and called for Dr. Schrager. We passed a few minutes in silence. Schrager came accompanied by Master Kamala.

"You nearly took a bite out of me before, mister," Schrager chided. "You got that shit under control?"

"For the moment," I said, shivering.

"Good news," he said.

Kamala stepped nearer and held my face in his hands, unafraid. He looked deep in my eyes, recalling that sense of communion from our first meeting.

"Well, my friend. It seems you've gotten yourself in a bit of a bind," he said. "Dr. Schrager and I have never had to deal with anything like this before."

"Stake me," I whispered, so only Kamala could hear. "It should work—there's blood in me now."

"If the time comes that we have lost all hope, I shall do this for you," he whispered back. "But that time is not yet."

"What have you come up with, Doc?" Garett asked.

Schrager leaned against a wall and lit a cigarette.

"We've got three ways to go with your friend here. One, we leave him alone to dry out. He seems to have been able to clean himself out before. We'd have to keep him isolated for a time, like a heroin addict, maybe sedated."

My throat tightened.

"As I understand it," I managed to say, "heroin addicts remain addicts, no matter how clean."

"That's true," he said. "But let's not second-guess it yet. This isn't heroin."

He took a drag off his cigarette.

"The second option is Kamala's idea," he continued calmly. "It's a little beyond me in its spiritual ramifications. We burn aspen into you, in the form of an inhalant."

"Inspired," I said. "What's option three?"

"We expose you to sunlight, to burn the blood out of you. It's what I would have recommended. But you appear capable of making your own decisions now, so the choice is yours." Seeing my horrified reaction, he added quickly, "In small doses, of course. Admittedly, it's quite dangerous."

The bastard would have left me delirious in the sun and taken notes while I writhed, I thought.

"How bad is it out there?" I asked Garett.

"Bad."

I turned to Kamala.

"Let's try it your way," I said.

They built the pyre a good ten feet high on the roof, beneath a crescent moon. The aspen logs had been airlifted in from upstate, the rooftop hastily fireproofed. At the center of the woodpile, they built a platform for me, just high enough to avoid the licking flames. It was a clear, windless night. Garett carried me up and set me on the platform. I dragged my legs into lotus position.

"Ready?" he said.

"Ready as I'm gonna be."

He climbed back down, lit a torch, and was about to insert it into the pyre when Kamala arrived.

"A moment please, Garett," he said, and climbed onto my platform.

"Mind if I join you?" he said.

"Very much," I responded. "This could be quite dangerous for you. You could get burned. Your lungs ... the smoke. Or I could lose control and kill you."

"How exciting," he said.

He assumed the lotus position, facing me; the platform's small size forced a kind of intimacy.

"Proceed," he called out.

Garett set the pyre aflame.

"Do you fear death, Master?" I said.

"I cherish it," he said. "I know that life continues after death."

My body shook hard as the first wisps of smoke reached

us. I tried breathing it in. This was quite difficult—I hadn't attempted inhaling since my death. I watched Kamala's gentle breathing—stomach inflating, chest rising, stomach pulling inward, smoke leaving the body through the nose motions—and tried to imitate them.

"I've spoken at length with Choi Leung," Kamala said. "He firmly believes you mastered the Art during a previous incarnation. Do you sense any truth in this?"

The smoke billowed up behind him now, the smell of the wood reminding me of when I built campfires with friends as kids upstate.

"An interesting development on that point," I said, pausing to inhale my first breath of the smoke. "I met the vampire who turned me. He said he'd only meant to drink from me. He was young, recently turned himself, I think. He said I reached up and seized the blood back, that he'd actually fought against it."

"As if you *chose* to turn yourself," he said.

The smoke was all around us now, the fire *crackling* louder. For Kamala's sake, I hoped the men below were keeping the flames in check. His eyes watered. He coughed several times. I moved to help him. He waved me away, regained control of his breath.

"I've walked on burning coals," he said. "Spent twenty days without nourishment. Scaled the Himalayas. I can endure this sacred smoke. How are you feeling, my friend?"

I inhaled a deep breath of smoke, feeling it inside me, in my nose, my mouth, my parched throat, and my long-unconsidered lungs.

"Maybe a little bit dizzy. The dominant sensation is still blood."

"You've brought a story to mind," he said. "May I tell it?"

"Please."

"In early eleventh-century Tibet lived a Master named Geshe Chekhawa. He was first and foremost a master of compassion. His most revered teaching was a practice for healing the sick called *tonglen*, in which we open our hearts to the afflicted and effect a transfer of our well-being for their ill health. A process I'm engaged in with you at this very moment. I'm centering my *tonglen* practice on finding the blood blocking your free flow of *pranic* energy, and trying to force it out of your body."

"Thank you, Master," I said. "But how?"

"I'm focusing my own *pranic* energy inside your body in search of the blood. Each time I encounter a blockage, I attempt to stir your *pranic* energy to remove it."

I thought of my experience after being turned.

"Does it appear that dark smoke is leaving my body, growing cleaner with each breath? As if the blockage were a lump of coal?"

Kamala smiled.

"Very astute. These are common visual manifestations of the *tonglen*."

I thought of Deirdre. Who had taught her these things? How would I ever know? Where was she now? I wished I could thank her for putting me onto the Path.

Kamala snapped me out of my reverie.

"Chekhawa searched far and wide for people in need of his healing, and found much success," he continued. "He healed thousands, yet his heart cried out to find those in greater need.

"Eventually he came to a colony of lepers and began to teach them the practice, working miracles of recovery and even cures. Lepers flocked to Chekhawa in droves, and with them came students of the *Way* who wished to learn his *tonglen*. He began teaching them, while still endeavoring to heal the world around him. As he neared the end of his life, he prayed to find his next rebirth in the Hell realms, to spread his compassion to those imprisoned there. He feared his prayers wouldn't be answered, and that he'd attain his rebirth in Nirvana, the realm of the Buddhas. He requested his students pray against this possibility. They acceded with tears in their eyes, praying their master's wish would be granted.

"I think you are like Geshe Chekhawa," Kamala concluded, his face darkened with soot. "That you've become what you are on purpose, and with purpose."

Blood tears fell from my eyes.

"Are you two all right?" Dr. Schrager called through the smoke.

"We survive," Kamala answered, his voice strong and clear. "I feel it is working."

Kamala's image blurred. Everything began spinning. Blood surged up from my stomach in spasms, burning all the way, and spewed out my mouth—onto the platform, myself, Kamala, and into the fire.

Garett helped us off the platform. Besides being covered in soot and blood vomit, Kamala looked no worse for wear. I continued vomiting onto the roof as Ministry men put out the fire.

Finally, I was just dry heaving. When that stopped, Dr. Schrager rolled me onto my back to examine me.

"He's lost a lot of his color," he told Garett. "I think that's a good sign."

He asked me how I felt.

"Weak," I said. "Empty."

"Good. Still want blood?"

I closed my eyes and looked inward, disgusted to find the blood wasn't completely gone.

"My body still wants it," I said.

"Then I recommend you meditate for the rest of the evening and unleash that voodoo you claim to have done in your apartment. Excuse me, I need to examine Kamala."

He stepped over me and walked off.

"He's really not such a bad guy," Garett said.

"Just a man with a grudge against vampires," I said. "I don't blame him."

We sat silently observing the moon, listening to the fire embers crackle.

"How many vampires were taken out in the rake?" I asked.

"Dozen or so."

"There were nearly a hundred at the ceremony."

"I know."

Garett was somber. He got up, dusted ashes from his jeans, looked out at the city.

"Daylight's a few hours off," he said. "Try to clear your head. We're gonna need you."

He left. I began chanting.

Om Mani Padme Hum. Om Mani Padme Hum.

Choi Leung floated into my thoughts, saying, "Once you've scaled this great mountain twice, you'll look back to see it was barely a hill."

Finally, I lost myself in the rhythm and slipped into emptiness.

I floated back into my body when one of the cleanup crew shouted sunrise was imminent. I sensed Kamala sitting nearby, in similar posture.

"Compassion," I said quietly. "Is that what slaying vampires is about?"

"For me, it has always been so," he said. "Saving people from them is a compassionate act, as is freeing vampires from themselves. You already know this."

"I think I begin to understand," I said.

"Good. How goes the dark diffusion?"

"Look in my eyes and see for yourself."

He gazed deep.

"There's still blood. Not a great deal, but ..."

I completed his thought.

"Enough to make us wonder if we can still be sure of me as a Slayer."

"Don't lose hope," Kamala said. "Tomorrow night ..."

"No," I said. "It's now or never. I have only one choice, if I'm ever going to feel safe again."

I got up, walked to the rooftop railing, and faced eastward. Kamala joined me, saying nothing, simply waiting with me as darkness gave way to light. The undersides of clouds whitened. The thin blue horizon line dividing sea and sky glimmered soft white. A few more seconds and the rim of the sun would appear and its life-giving beams lash out at me.

I felt compelled to rush inside and cower—no doubt the blood at work—but fought it. If this was my last dance, it was beautiful. Miraculous.

The sun edged over the horizon. The first shafts of light flashed straight at me like razorblades to a magnet, their intensity forcing my eyes shut. Kamala's hands on my shoulders steadied me.

"Face it!" he whispered. "Open your eyes!"

I forced my eyes open.

Sunlight blasted my bare face and hands—pain unmatched by any I'd ever felt or have since experienced. My screams were so piercing, the crew had to cover their ears. My body convulsed. I felt I was about to burst into flames when suddenly I knew all the sun wanted was the blood.

It took what it wanted, dropping me to my knees, burning, burning, an ecstasy of pain in every fiber of my body, until I was emptied. No drop of blood remained.

In a haze, I felt a blanket or something thrown over my head and several sets of hands dragging me inside the building.

17

R eproduction is a basic *pranic* instinct that may not be denied in any species except Man, and Man's development beyond this physiological drive is a very recent occurrence. Nowhere in the animal kingdom do animals seek to curb the growth and spread of the lifeforce. But Man desires to control, to manipulate, and in certain situations, to dement the transference process.

How does the vampire's reproductive instinct arise? What sparks them to rove amok in packs during the Black Season, not killing their victims but transforming them? The answer to this koan may someday extinguish the vampire as a human subspecies, and subsequently, the Art itself.

———

I LEARNED LATER from the crew that I'd been laughing when they grabbed me—laughter the likes of which they'd never heard before. Kamala confirmed this, adding that when he'd asked me if indeed the blood was out, and if that was the source of my good humor, I'd replied, "It's a gate. The sun's a gate."

I had to take his word for it.

I woke that evening in my quarters, free of blood yet forever tainted, aware that the knowledge I was accumulating was not for the Ministry's good but *for the good of the Vampire.* (I'll be impressed if the Ministry doesn't strike that statement from this work.)

With resurrected vigor, I dressed in my *kesa* and headed for the command post for a report on the state of the city. I wanted to see status reports on every city worldwide, wanted all the raw data the Ministry had collected on vampire incidence in its dozens of musty storerooms, hoping to figure out what factors led to a Black Season, and set us on course to prevent it—to discover, in effect, some method of vampire birth control.

Detecting the scent of the *un*dead as I left the Slayers' barracks, I concluded someone must've been down here prior to decontamination with bloodied remains on their gear. Still, it was worth reporting.

The command post was buzzing with activity. Dozens of Ministry personnel milled about, many of whom I'd never seen before. Some sat swilling coffee; others paced. A few Slayers from other districts looked at me warily. Clearly we were gearing up for something big.

Garett was at a desk in a corner, phone to his ear. He waved me toward him. I heard the tail end of his conversation.

"... and infrared. I need forty. ASAP. Thanks."

"Evening," I said.

"Evening."

Dark circles ringed his blue eyes. He looked like he'd aged ten years overnight.

"Big show, huh?" he said. "Forty-two Slayers, two Masters on the premises. You up for a big rake, find that strigoi of yours?"

"I'm in."

"You ready for this?"

"I'm clean, if that's what you're asking. Where's the deployment?"

"We think they're holed up in the sewers. Can you imagine?"

"It's an ideal locale for a den—unlimited space, zero sunlight, citywide access. How did we come to think this?"

"This morning, city workers making repairs beneath the Village found three bodies with nasty throats. Called it in to police and we interceded. I sent a day team to take water, air, pollutant samples. They say the chance of a den is in the upper eightieth percentile. Kamala called for all available personnel."

Garett's rapid heart rate and slight face blanching indicated there was something else he wanted to say.

"What are you holding back?" I said.

His jaw tightened.

"Not here," he mouthed.

I followed him into the corridor.

"Heard you stepped out in the sun," he said.

"You hear right. I think in time I'll be able to remain in direct sunlight indefinitely."

"Do you think a *cure* is possible?"

"I don't know. There'll have to be tests."

"But what do you *think*, damn it?"

I'd never seen him so unnerved.

"What's wrong, Garett?"

I reached out. He brushed my hand off his shoulder, shook his head, raised his hands in the air in frustration.

"Did you, or did you not, actually *see* Craig die?" he said.

"What are you looking for, Garett? Revenge? Because I know the one who did it."

"Just answer me!"

"I didn't see him die. The strigoi took him to another room, after torturing him in front of me. Craig never broke down. He was defiant to the last. What is it you want to know?"

He kicked his boot heel against the wall in frustration.

"I think Craig's been turned. We didn't find his body. The morning we rescued you, I noticed his door had been left open. Something made me go in. I felt his presence, like he'd just been there. I chalked it up to wishful thinking. I sat on his bed for a while, looked at the photos on his desk—his parents, his sister who died. I didn't want to be in there, believe me, but I forced myself and said my goodbyes. His death was my responsibility, my ..."

"Bullshit," I said. "I'm the one who broke direct orders and brought him in. If anyone's responsible, it's me."

"No," he said. "He was a Slayer and that's that. He risked his neck every damned night, more than any of us. And nothing was going to stop you from going in there. Kamala and I both knew that. Craig knew it, too. We saw what was coming, and chose not to intervene. That's my responsibility. I should've been planning with you, not just shadowing you."

He stopped, took a breath.

"Let me finish what I was trying to tell you," he started again, his tone relaxed. "I didn't get much sleep after that.

Then we had to deal with getting you back on your feet. But something nagged at me. I went back to his room. Something was missing. Care to guess what?"

"A Stake?"

"Not just one. He kept four in a rack above his bed. Each one belonged to a Slayer lost since he'd signed on. All four were gone. I don't know how I missed them, the first time."

I remembered Alexis placing Craig's Stake into his crippled hand. What if that hand had been transformed? Who would he turn it on?

"What does Kamala say?"

"He doesn't know what I suspect. You're the only one I've told."

"Why me?"

He locked eyes with me.

"If Craig's out there, turned, he's a Wild Stake—a threat to them and us. Our orders are to slay with extreme prejudice. Too many Ministry agents have gone down at the hands of a Wild Stake they thought they could handle. Understand now?"

"You want to know whether I can save him, make him like me. That is, if we can get to him before one of the others Stakes him."

"Can you?"

"I honestly don't know, Garett. If he's turned, I don't know how far it's gone. Has he tasted blood yet? Killed anyone? He could be wandering the streets in a blood craze. I'm not even sure *I'm* safe, this time."

"There's something else I haven't told you," Garett said. "I was down in the sewers inspecting the death site, and flipped on a tracer."

"Craig and I were both wearing them."

"Yours was still activated when we got you out. That's how we found you. I thought ..."

"Craig might still have his. Was there a signal?"

"A weak one, further down the tunnels. But it wasn't moving. What do you think?"

"I think you should reconsider telling Kamala and warning the other Slayers, before we head in."

"I'll take that under advisement."

He thanked me then walked back to the control room alone.

H oly War.

The Ministry records each vampire encounter as either a victory or a defeat in a Holy War. In joining the Ministry, Aspirants of the Art of Slaying Vampires pledge themselves to this Holy War and sharing the resulting group karma.

The image of Holy War depicted in the Old Testament isn't attractive. According to the book of Deuteronomy, the wandering Hebrew nation, carrying the Ark of the Covenant, engaged in what they saw as Holy Wars against their enemies, commanded by God to "save alive nothing that breathes: But utterly destroy them."

When seizing an enemy city, they slaughtered every man, woman, and child regardless of resistance, then slaughtered every animal, believing the enemy was an infection to the body, the "community," capable of spreading corruption to the host by its mere presence.

The Ministry interprets the edict "Sacrifice even your own liberation until all sentient beings are free from suffering" to require that *all* vampires be slain in order to ensure the ascension of Mankind, comparable to a doctor amputating a cancerous limb to save a patient's life: drastic but necessary.

Holy War is the koan with which I constantly struggle.

———

AT 4:00 AM three teams of fourteen Ministry operatives apiece went down into the sewer tunnels beneath Manhattan, deploying at separate entry points, to triangulate toward the main concourse junction. Team One was led by Kamala, Team Two by Master Dau Chen.

Garett led our Team Three in at midtown off Sixth Avenue. The temperature dropped drastically as we descended the service ladder into pitch darkness. The first thing I noticed was the pervasive sound of running water, moving, slithering, echoing. It seemed the whole place was alive. At the foot of the ladder the concrete floors were submerged in about six inches of acrid mucky water. Everyone was dressed in waterproof thermal gear and armed with Stakes, military grade flamethrowers, and headsets.

"Welcome to the Metropolitan Sewer System, people," came Garett's voice in our ears. "Goggles on. Go night vision."

He handed me a pair of goggles. I put them on, looked around, passed them back.

"I'm better without them," I said. "If the vampires see what I see, you guys have about a fifteen-percent handicap."

"No shit?" said a Slayer named Gilbert.

"No shit," I said. "Everybody should get a bead on me."

Garett switched channels on his radio.

"Team Three is in," he reported. "Repeat, Team Three is in. How copy?"

"Copy, Team Three, this is Team Two," came the static-filled response. "We're in position and moving out. No incidence."

"Copy, Team Two and Team Three. Team One in position. No incidence," came Kamala's voice. "Proceed with caution."

Garett led us progressively down a series of rusted staircases through the sewer tunnels. A Slayer named Erickson called coordinates off a map he referenced. Water beaded and streamed along the walls.

"Great setting for a horror film," Gilbert commented.

"I'm smelling vampires, gentlemen," I announced via my headset.

"Activate 'throwers," Garett ordered.

Thirteen fire streams illuminated the tunnel—for obvious reasons, I wasn't carrying one—reflecting in the water we sloshed through and casting our shadows against the mold-covered walls.

"Hold up," called one of the Slayers ahead of me. "I just tripped on something."

He reached into the water, lifted out a badly decomposed human leg, severed near the thigh, and cast it away.

"Team Three has a death site," Garett called into his set. "How copy?"

"Copy," Team One responded.

"Copy," echoed Team Two.

We moved on. The water deepened to knee level, slowing our progress. I moved up to Garett, who held a tracer in his hand. It was silent. We shared a look. He switched it off and pocketed it.

"Worth a try," he said. Then, into his set: "No lights on our potential Wild Stake."

Erickson consulted his map as we approached a shaft in the tunnel.

"Down," he said.

The air carried a thick scent of sulfur in the lower tunnel.

"Crates ... hundreds of 'em! ... Definitely a den!" Team Two transmitted, the Slayer's voice distorted by static.

"Come back, Team Two, we're not reading you clearly," Garett called into his set. "You say you've got coffins, confirm? How copy?"

"We can hear them, Team Three," Kamala responded from Team One. "Switch to channel five and I'll relay what they're saying."

We switched over. Kamala continued to communicate between both teams.

"Team Two is opening one of the caskets. Copy that? They say they have a vampire submerged in blood. Slain. I repeat, it has been staked."

"Copy, Team One," Garett said. "Give us coordinates for Team Two."

"They're one floor beneath Main Concourse, Junction Five. They report half-a-dozen caskets with slain occupants. The rest are empty. Proceed with caution. Incidence appears imminent."

"Let's move out," Garett called. "Erickson, point us the way."

Erickson swiftly moved down the tunnel; we kept pace behind him. The water climbed to thigh level. A familiar, rotten smell assaulted me.

"Heads up, I smell blood, gentlemen," I called over my set.

Erickson's sharp gasp reverberated through our headsets as he and Garett rounded a corner ahead of us, out of sight. A moment later we found them frozen in their tracks. The tunnel ahead was blocked with human corpses, hung by ropes and hooks from the ceiling and walls like in a meat locker, in various states of decay. Hundreds of them, enough to close the greater portion of New York City's missing persons files, and then some.

"Any other way down there, Erickson?" Garett called into his set.

"Back the way we came," he said, consulting his map. "Or plow on through this."

A Slayer from Team Two yelled into our ears through a hail of static.

"*Un*dead coming out of their crates! Get the fuck down here!"

"We're going through," Garett ordered. "Let's move!"

We forced a path with our hands and elbows. Each time one of us pushed a body aside to step clear, it swung back maddeningly against the man behind us.

"Keep your heads, gentlemen, they're just trees," Garett called. "Branches of trees brushing up against us as we stroll through the woods."

I couldn't accept his suggestion. These had been human beings, men, women, and children. There were more bodies underwater we had to step on to move ahead. And the smell ...

Finally, we broke through. We stopped for one man to vomit, then moved on at breakneck speed.

"They should be just ahead!" Erickson called. "Main Concourse Junction Five is just above us."

"Throwers ready," Garett ordered. "Good hunting!"

A swarm of vampires sped toward us. Six went down shrieking in flames. A seventh eluded the fire and rushed Erickson, who hadn't drawn a weapon. I lunged between them and smashed the vampire in the chest. It clawed the air as it went down.

We fled the tunnel, into the main concourse, an enormous industrial chamber serving as a terminal for dozens of tunnels. The sound of thrashing pumps and rushing water was pervasive, now and again overcome by vampire or human shrieks. There were stairways up, down, and lengthwise across the vast man-made cavern, and a catwalk running the length of the high ceiling.

I rushed headlong into the battle in progress. Here are glimpses of what I saw when not surrendering to the killing ground myself, slaying vampires with my hand.

A Slayer named Thompkins impaled a vampire against a wall, tore his Stake free, and impaled another. Three vampires disemboweled a Slayer I didn't know. Garett set two vampires ablaze with his flamethrower.

A vampire fleeing a Slayer leaped down from two floors above me, shattering bones as it crashed into the cement floor. Another Slayer moved in and torched it as it lay flailing.

Somewhere behind me a human scream stopped short after a flamethrower hit.

Master Dau Chen rushed up a ladder onto a platform where two blood-drenched Slayers retreated before five vampires, discharging blue-white light from his body like pulse beats as he moved between the wounded Slayers and their attackers. The vampires turned to Dau Chen. He steepled his hands over his chest. A dazzle of light, a blur of motion, and the vampires went up in flames.

A vampire who couldn't have been more than ten years old when she'd been turned lunged for my throat, slashing at my face as I swung for her chest, struck, and beat her aside.

Garett was up on a catwalk, shouting something to a Slayer far below him at a tunnel mouth. The man stepped out of sight. An old female vampire dressed like a nurse lunged at me out of nowhere while I was distracted, sank her teeth into my neck. I tore her off me, ripping away some of my skin—in her mouth, under her nails. I cried out in pain as she threw herself at me again. I slashed out and took her down then rushed to help an unknown Slayer whose left arm was practically severed, but got there too late. I slew the vampire that killed him and said a death prayer as I moved on.

I slew and I slew, taking out vampires until I'd cleared a wide circle around me. I moved to assist a few pockets of combat nearby as Master Dau Chen led a group of four Slayers off the concourse, down one of the tunnels.

Then I saw Craig, a Stake in each hand, bounding up a flight of stairs toward the upper levels.

My eyes followed his upward course to his destination: an open hatch where Alexis stood surveying the battle below, apparently unaware Craig was heading toward him and the vampire beside him (either Siobhan or Corinne).

"Garett," I yelled in my set. "Craig and the strigoi, twelve o'clock high!"

I spotted him two levels above me.

"Got them. On my way!"

I broke into a run, dodging fire jets as I went. Craig was going to reach Alexis first, with Garett only moments behind him. I feared for both their safety.

I moved up the stairs with a speed I'd never known, taking them five, six at a time, ascending in veritable leaps. Alexis moved back into the tunnel, out of sight. Craig was nearly upon him. I couldn't see Garett. Three more flights. Two. One. I hit the landing and rounded the corner too quickly, skidding hard into a wall. It took me a moment to regain my footing and continue at a dead run.

I heard voices up ahead, then a scream, then the jet of a flamethrower. At the end of the tunnel, I stepped into some sort of relay room. Alexis stood near the center, holding a gun to a human girl's head. Garett was against a wall, his left shoulder bloody, exposed through his bodysuit, his hands gripping his flamethrower tightly, aiming alternately at Alexis then Craig, who was circling Alexis, a Stake in each hand. He had blood in him—a great deal of it—confirming he'd been turned.

"Welcome," Alexis called as I stepped in. "Just what we needed, a fifth player. I think you know everybody."

Craig glanced at me with tormented eyes. He seemed incapable of communication. I sensed very little of Craig left in him. Blood saliva dripped from his lips as he bared his teeth. Suddenly he turned his attention from me and lunged at Alexis.

Alexis shot Craig in the chest with two loud bursts. Craig reeled backward into a corner, crumpling to his knees in rasping moans.

Alexis chuckled.

"*Oooh*, painful," he sneered.

Meanwhile his claws remained tight on the girl's throat. I recognized her with shock—the girl whose blood he'd injected into my veins. She had dozens of raw bite marks now, on her neck, down her arms. She moaned weakly, made a pathetic attempt to pull free.

The sight and the scent of her threw me. I desperately needed her out of there. I'd be fine with anyone else, but not her.

Alexis smiled evilly.

"She was yours once."

Garett stood against the wall, flamethrower lit, aimed low, finger cool on the trigger. Watching us.

Craig sprang back up, blood in his eyes, Stakes whirling in his hands. Alexis looked at him anxiously. I realized it was Craig who'd staked all those vampires in their coffins.

"Keep that one back," Alexis demanded, indicating Craig. "Or I kill the girl."

"Craig, stand down!" Garett called.

Craig looked at Garett, his eyes wild, Stakes twirling, then back at Alexis.

"He doesn't hear you, Garett," I said. "Look at his eyes. He's turned. He's full of blood, in pain. He can't see the girl for what she is. She's like a paper shield between him and the one who gave him that pain."

"How eloquent," Alexis said, digging a fingernail into the girl's neck, drawing blood, his gun aimed at Garett.

He turned to me.

"Either I get out of here without pursuit or I kill both of *these*," he said, indicating Garett and the girl.

Craig inched forward, ready to pounce. Garett saw it, too, and triggered a fire jet in his path. Craig recoiled, hissing and spitting, his hair singed.

This could be the blackest gate of Garett's life, I thought.

"Craig, *stand down!*" Garett repeated. Then, to Alexis:

"Release the girl, and you walk. One more drop of blood comes out of her, I'll fry you to cinders."

Alexis ignored Garett, confident he wouldn't trigger the flamethrower while he held the girl, assured it would keep Craig at bay. He looked at me, unsure where I stood.

"Well, my Dark Brother," he said, his punctured lips curled in a sneer. "Does she live or die?"

I looked at her face. There was so much pain, so much terror. Bloodied swathes of blonde hair fell around the face of an angel. She was part of my damnation and always would be; her lifeblood had been in me. Her glazed green eyes looked at me, pleading to be set free.

Was I imagining it?

Don't give up, I silently cried out to her. *I can still save you.*

You must set me free, came her response. *Can't you see I'm finished here? You have my forgiveness.*

"Alexis, my Dark Brother," I said calmly. "There's no way you're getting out of here. Let her go and give yourself up. Or just kill her now and let's finish this."

His sneer faded; hatred burned in his stare. He bared his fangs.

Suddenly Craig lunged. I dodged in front of him; the killing ground reached out through my hand and I slammed his chest. Alexis shot Garett. Craig shrieked and planted a Stake in my chest. I crashed backward against a wall, sliding downward as Garett collapsed across from me. A Stake *in* my chest! *Satori.*

Alexis shot two more rounds into Craig, to no effect. Craig whisked the girl away in a stream of blood, reached out from his own killing ground, and drove his remaining Stake into Alexis's heart, wrenched it free, drove it in again, then stepped back and wailed in agony.

Alexis looked at me with disbelief before he exploded, splattering the relay room with blood.

Craig went down—hard. The bullets had torn his chest badly, but that wound could heal. Suddenly I hoped I hadn't struck him true.

Garett crawled over to me and examined the Stake half-embedded in my breastbone.

"It's in deep," he said. "You gonna make it?"

"No blood, no ignition," I managed. "It hurts a lot, though."

The girl moaned. Garett crawled to her. She wasn't dead, but close.

Craig crawled slowly to a corner of the room, trailing blood, and propped himself against the wall, the rage gone from his features. He looked serene.

"Garett," he called out, his voice rich with vampiric resonance. "Scorched 'em again, didn't we? Raked the bastards!"

He turned his attention to me.

"Want to know what it's like?"

I nodded.

"It's like the desire for blood just drains off, goes away somewhere. You're still hungry but not that way. I can see Garett, the girl, even you so clearly now, not like a human, not like a vampire, but clearly. That's what you do to them. You open their eyes and they can't help realize what they've become."

"Thank you, Craig," I said.

Garett moved to Craig, knelt close beside him. The wounds on Craig's chest were healing. The bullet appeared to have passed through Garett's right shoulder.

"Can he be saved?" Garett asked, his voice thick with emotion. "Can you clean him out?"

"The only one who knows the answer to that is him," I said.

Craig looked at Garett and smiled.

"I'm good to go, pal."

Garett's features softened; he returned his attention to the girl.

"We need a medical unit, Stat! Three down. Top level, Relay Room!" he called into his headset.

Within minutes there were footfalls fast approaching. Several Ministry men rushed into the room, looking like they'd been through hell.

"We won!" Gilbert shouted. "Raked every damned one of 'em!"

"Get that medical team in here!" Garett said, rising up on shaky legs. "Save your victory cry till the wounded are seen to."

"They're on their way," Gilbert said, growing somber as he surveyed the room.

Craig raised his hand to me and mouthed, "Goodbye."

We locked eyes; I sent him all the courage and compassion I could muster, silently saying a Tibetan prayer for his safe journey.

Craig flared out, his soul lighting off for the frontier in a sheet of flame. In moments, he was ash.

Garett looked at me accusingly, his face a mask of anguish.

"What the fuck just happened?"

"He'd killed too many," I said. "He couldn't tell you that. I think he was strong enough to pull through physically if I hadn't struck him true, but he knew he could never atone for the guilt."

Dr. Schrager came rushing in then, took one look at the Stake in my chest, and grinned.

"Nice!"

"Over here, Doc," Garett called. "I really need you to save the girl."

DR. SCHRAGER REMOVED the Stake from my body, telling jokes throughout the surgery. The wound healed nicely. It was all meticulously captured on film. Lying on the operating table, conscious of each incision, every probe, and a plethora of splinters, I fell into a dream.

I was sitting at the center of a small circle of people—some humans and a few vampires, all my students—illustrating the place in my chest where the Stake had penetrated. We were seated in the sand on a beach by a clear sea, beneath a warm sun. One student raised his hand.

"Get ready, it's coming out now!" he said when I acknowledged him.

Suddenly I felt wrenching pain from the wound. My eyes shut tight then reopened upon Choi Leung, standing before me smiling with delight.

"Look!" he yelled, indicating a grand, ornate mirror hanging in the air, its surface rippling like water yet reflecting Choi Leung's image.

I was unsettled to see I cast no reflection.

"It's out!" Choi Leung whispered, and burst into laughter.

"It's out!" Schrager announced.

Waking, I looked up to see him stripping off his gloves.

"The wound's already healed itself," he said. "Keep the bandage on for a few hours. I'll bill you."

Two evenings later a funeral service was held at the upstate monastery for the eleven Slayers who'd perished in the sewers. Boston sent personnel to watch over the city while we attended. Three bodies were on hand; the others had been shipped home to loved ones with cover stories concealing the actual cause of death. It was quite a beautiful service, with Garett and Kamala delivering closing prayers. (Garett had previously visited Craig's parents, explaining only as much as the Ministry permitted and disobeying orders by allowing them to keep Craig's ashes.)

I said my own prayers then, finally, for my parents, Chelsea, Deirdre, and the girl who in the end couldn't be saved, whose name I later learned but won't record here. Afterward I found myself strolling among the flowers in the garden with Choi Leung, discussing recent events.

"The Ministry has decided to disseminate knowledge of the Art," he said. "It's time."

"I think that's wise," I said. "The public needs this information."

"I'm glad you agree," he said, grinning like the Cheshire Cat. "I've recommended that you write the treatise."

I laughed.

"Why would you recommend me?"

He placed his hands on my shoulders.

"You've been educated in Western thought," he said. "You write well, and you're the only one who can deliver a full account from both sides of the fence, so to speak."

"The Ministry might not appreciate everything I'd have to say on the subject."

"Something troubles you, my friend," he said, his expression solemn. "Please share it with me."

"A dream I keep having," I said.

"Tell me."

I recounted the dream about standing with him before the mirror, my casting no reflection, and him laughing at me.

Choi Leung burst into gleeful laughter.

"The dawning is nearly upon you!" he exclaimed.

Chapter Under Consideration
For Omission Pending Ministry Approval.

Authorial Intent Unclear

Inevitably, the Vampire must be saved if Mankind is to ascend beyond its present state of karmic disarray. By "saved" I do not refer to either *spared* as it is defined in the traditional sense, nor to the Christian definition of *saved*, in that some act of contrition must be sought and employed.

All of the killing must end.

It must, for surely the Slayers themselves cannot shoulder these karmic blows indefinitely, no matter how pure of heart they may become. We are fighting negative based energy with negative based energy here, against beings who, although technically clinically deceased, are without any doubt sentient beings. We, in retribution against their crimes with the driving of the Stake, are clearly breaking the edict of the First Law of the *Way: Be as if one with all life.* Thus, we must regress to the original dilemma the Masters suffered centuries before us; the Vampire *is* a natural predator of Man—from where do we garner the right to destroy him? To say that Vampires who prey on *prana* chance encountering *prana* that preys on Vampires is not sufficient.

At present, this edict which founded our branch of the sect is a necessity. I don't propose we allow vampires to breed worldwide. Nonetheless, I find the Ministry guilty of stagnation within the edict, in its failure to seek out the further spiritual growth so obviously required.

We cannot let the Vampire overtake Mankind, for the bulk of Mankind is clearly a step ahead on the path to universal enlightenment. Still, the Vampire *is* a subspecies of Man, and eventually must be numbered among the enlightened for us to truly "sacrifice even our own liberation until all sentient beings are free from suffering."

The very term "Blackened Gate" reads volumes into my argument, for is this gate not *blackened* due to the obvious karmic ramifications upon the man who would traverse this gate seeking exaltation as a slayer of sentient life?

I fear we are caught up in a game of lesser evils here. Freeing a vampire from suffering is surely an act of true compassion, requiring no justification, but this is merely the treatment of a symptom rather than a true attempt to combat the root of the disease gripping our society. Safeguarding the *prana* of future victims has become a weak shield behind which we hide.

The Initiation of the Stake was meant to be a temporary solution at best, and should be warranted only for the coming generation and perhaps the generation after it. This perpetual circle of violence must end, and vampires must be returned to the fold. Shall we, already on the Path, not make ourselves tools to facilitate this reinstatement? All Mankind would benefit.

I predict that the Ministry, as it presently stands, shall collapse within no longer than a century's time. Its fate rests in its own hands. Due to my personal ethics, I cannot remain an active agent.

I hereby secede from my post as a Ministry operative.

I leave you in peace with this koan:

If you meet the Vampire upon the path, you have but two choices: Slay him or slay him not.
Slay him not and surely he shall slay you.
But I warn you, if you slay him you shall surely slay yourself.

Good Hunting.

ABOUT THE AUTHOR

Steven-Elliot Altman is a best-selling author, graphic novelist, ADDY Award-Winning advertising executive, television writer-producer, and most recently a successful videogame developer, having served as the Games Director at Acclaim  Games, and having won multiple awards for the games he has penned which include such titles as: *9Dragons*, which boasts 15 million players; *Pearl's Peril*, which boasts 90 million players; *Ancient Aliens: The Game* and *Project Blue Book: Hidden Mysteries* which Steve wrote, produced, and narrative designed for the History Channel, based on two of their hit television series. His latest game is *Terminator: Dark Fate*, based on the feature film.

Steve's novels include *Captain America Is Dead*, *Zen in the Art of Slaying Vampires*, *Batman: Fear Itself*, *The Killswitch Review*, *The Irregulars*, *Deprivers*, and *Severed Wings*. He's also the editor of the critically acclaimed anthology *The Touch*, and a contributor to *Shadows Over Baker Street*, a Hugo Award-Winning anthology of Sherlock Holmes stories. Steve's also a proud member of the Science Fiction & Fantasy Writers of America, the Horror Writers Association, and is the current Vice-Chairman of the steering committee of the Writers Guild of America's Videogame Division.

When Steve's not writing he is often playing social games with strange and wondrous people on and off of airplanes between Los Angeles, New York, and Berlin.

IF YOU LIKED …

If you liked *Zen in the Art of Slaying Vampires,*
you might also enjoy:

Dan Shamble, Zombie P.I. Zomnibus

by Kevin J. Anderson

Season of the Wolf

by Jeff Marriotte

OTHER WORDFIRE PRESS TITLES BY STEVEN-ELLIOT ALTMAN

Severed Wings

Our list of other WordFire Press authors and titles is always growing. To find out more and to see our selection of titles, visit us at:

wordfirepress.com

f facebook.com/WordfireIncWordfirePress

🐦 twitter.com/WordFirePress

📷 instagram.com/WordFirePress

BB bookbub.com/profile/4109784512

www.ingramcontent.com/pod-product-compliance
Lightning Source LLC
Chambersburg PA
CBHW050330110726
47899CB00007B/2439